專門替中國人寫的
英文課本 高級本 上

1片朗讀光碟
1片互動光碟

李家同/策劃・審訂

文庭澍/著

暨南大學
多媒體與通訊實驗室/光碟製作

序

李家同

　　我一直認為我們該教英文文法的，理由很簡單，我們大多數人沒有說英文的環境，因此孩子們是不會自動說好英文的。舉例來說，很多孩子在用過去式的時候喜歡用 verb to be 的過去式，我日前看到一個孩子寫出了 "I was saw a bird"。我指出他的錯誤以後，他承認這是他很早以前所寫的，現在他已不會再犯這種錯誤了。

　　但是他忽然問我：「那什麼時候我們會用was呢？」我告訴他一個例子，"He was a teacher before." 他才恍然大悟。

　　我們必須承認我們中國人所犯的英文文法錯誤，都是英語母語人士不會犯的。我敢說，教育程度再差的美國孩子，也不會說出 "I was not go to school yesterday." 所以適合我們的文法書必須要針對中國人的需求來寫。

　　文庭澍老師寫的《專門替中國人寫的英文課本》（高級本上冊）出爐了，這本書主要的內容仍然是文法，但是文老師寫這本書採用了非常特別的方法：

(1) 她仍然將我們中國人所常犯的文法錯誤指出來了。舉例來說，我們對詞性向來大而化之，該用動詞的時候，卻常常用成名詞。我的學生就經常犯這種錯誤。

(2) 她用文章來教文法,這是完全正確的作法,看了文章以後,就更能
　　了解文法的意義。

(3) 這本書仍然有大量的練習,有改錯,也有中翻英,這些對增進英文
　　能力來說,都是非常有意義的。

作者自序

文庭澍

2003和2004兩年的暑假，我在李家同校長指導下，一口氣寫完了《專門為中國人寫的英文課本》初、中級本一系列共四本書。這套書在當時以全英文「溝通式教學法」為主流的英文市場是個異數，但很快地便從讀者熱烈的迴響中，我們看出這套大量使用中文說明及強調文法重要性的課本有其基本需求，不但能使許多英文初學者以及在學習英文這條路上跌跌撞撞的學習者重拾信心，更能補「溝通式教學法」之不足。

寫完這四本書後，常常收到讀者來信，有些點出錯誤、有些則討論文法規則背後的理由；每次讀者來信，我必嚴肅以待，仔細回答。最近一年來，讀者的來信多詢問高級本何時出書，許多讀者已將初、中級本四本作業都做完了，很想循序漸進，再用高級本來繼續挑戰自己的能力。我自己對高級本已有基本構想，遲遲未動手的原因是考慮讓讀者慢慢消化四本，不必一次出齊六本，使讀者心生壓力。但近幾個月來，由於讀者和出版社不斷「施壓」，我開始認真地從讀者來信中構思高級本的明確方向。和李教授討論的結果，我們一致認為高級本不能和初、中級本一樣只有短句和會話；應以文章的型態出現，且每篇文章都應包括複雜的句型，終究日常生活中會用到的英文句型不只包含主詞、動詞和受詞而已，通常還包含許多子句及複雜的概念，一味學習簡單句型，讀者的英文能力是無法提升的。但適合讀者閱讀的文章要去哪裡找呢？整本書的主軸又該如何定位呢？

　　以我自己這幾年在大學教授大一英文、英文作文與英文新聞閱讀的經驗，發覺當今由美語班訓練而長大的學生，聽力是有些微進步，也能不怕生地開口說幾句美語，但文法觀念卻一落千丈，英文程度稍差的連《專門為中國人寫的英文課本》初級本的基本概念都不清楚，令人吃驚的是英文中上程度的學生也不知詞類變化為何物，交來的英文作業觸目皆是 "I am health." "It is convenience." "My interesting is playing computer games." 之類的錯誤句子。最難忘的例子是某位學生寫的下面這個句子：The food is deliciously. 當問及何以用副詞deliciously形容名詞food，該生的回答居然是：「形容詞放在句尾時，不是都該加ly嗎？」同樣的情形還發生在一位寫了 "My happy is..." 的學生身上，當問到何以所有格代名詞My後面只接形容詞，該生反問：「不用形容詞要用什麼詞呢？」我搖首嘆息之餘，決定要利用高級本把各種詞類用最簡單的文字，說清楚、講明白。

　　主軸確定後，接下來該決定每一課課文以何種方法呈現？我發現一般英文課本不是以漫畫呈現課文，就是獨立的一課一文，而課文與課文之間互不相連。為了增加讀者的好奇心，我決定以連續劇的方式編寫故事，一課一段情節，情節圍繞在三個主要角色（已退休的老爸、快退休的老媽和即將考大學的兒子）的日常生活打轉。選這幾個年齡層的理由是，從讀者來信中發現其中不乏中年退休人士和年輕學子，他們也許能從主角的生活點滴中得到角色認同感。各課課文除了以情節取勝外，另有其文法的功能與目的，如第四課談的是動詞片語，大量的動詞片語如：pick up, dig in, tidy up等紛紛出籠，第七課主題是副詞，課文中不乏副詞的特殊用法。希望可使讀者在閱讀課文之餘，不知不覺中了解該課所闡述的文法規則。

　　另外，為了使課文實用且生動有趣，我不斷尋找與當今社會相關的議題，如終生學習（lifelong learning）、兩性平等（gender equality）、愛護動物（animal protection）、環境保護（environmental protection）、節省能源（energy saving）等，使讀者不但能學到各類英文字彙，還能了解社會脈動與全世界所關注的焦點所在。

　　和前四本書一樣，高級本每課先來一段導言，導言中鮮少難懂的專有名詞，而是用最簡單的話把複雜的文法概念說清楚。每一課課文都有課文解析，遇到讀者易出錯的地方，特別以「注意」標明，詳加解釋以提醒讀者。此外，每課課文後會附上大量習題，供讀者反覆演練，讀者自習的過程中如果發現自己的答案與書中的答案有出入，但不了解錯在哪裡，請寫email到wentingshu@gmail.com，我一定會盡快回答。

　　這套書的完成須感謝李家同教授確立寫書的大方向，李教授雖不是我英語教學的同行，但給我的啟發，遠超過同行的大師。我的子姪們：Christian Nordin,　Rachel Lin, Karen Lin, Yvonne Yeh, Miranda Lin等人幫我潤稿：老友，也是與我合著《用英文說台灣》一書的作者Cathy Dibell以及負責校稿的Chris Findler先生提供不少寶貴的意見，最後再加上聯經出版公司何采嬪和林雅玲的編輯專業，使這本書增色不少，當然還須加上讀者日後不斷的來信指教，定能使這套書更臻完美。

目 次

序 .... 李家同　　i

作者自序 .... 文庭澍　　iii

第一課　　詞類變化──名詞 1

第二課　　詞類變化──動名詞 17

第三課　　動詞──三態變化 35

第四課　　動詞──動詞片語 55

第五課　　動詞──容易混淆的動詞 69

第六課　　形容詞 87

第七課　　副詞 109

第八課　　助動詞 125

附　　錄 147

總複習 152

習題解答 159

總複習解答 171

第一課 Unit 1

詞類變化——名詞

互動光碟

　　詞類變化是學生學英文所遇到最大的瓶頸之一，我們在中級本第八課已釐清了一些詞類變化的基本觀念，例如什麼時候用名詞、什麼時候用形容詞、什麼時候用動詞、什麼時候用副詞，不過許多讀者反應，詞類變化還是很令人頭痛。現在以 safety（安全）這個字為例，說明這個字的各種詞類變化及其用法：

🎧 <u>Safety</u> is our primary concern.
安全是我們的首要考量。
safety 是名詞。

🎧 I feel <u>safe</u>.
我覺得安全。
safe 是形容詞。

🎧 He <u>saves</u> NT$1000 every month.
他每個月存台幣1000元。
save 是動詞。

🎧 You had better drive <u>safely</u>.
你最好小心開車。
safely 是副詞。

　　高級本（上冊）將介紹一系列詞類變化，首先介紹名詞，接著介紹動詞、形容詞和副詞，並詳細說明每種詞類的特性和用法。

　　首先我們先介紹名詞。名詞是人、動物、東西和地方的名稱。名詞可分為以下五類：

🎧 1. 普通名詞，如 book（書）, student（學生）, flower（花）。
🎧 2. 集合名詞，如 class（班級）, group（團體）, family（家庭）。
🎧 3. 專有名詞，如 Wendy（溫蒂）, Taiwan（台灣）, McDonald's（麥當勞）。

🎵 4.物質名詞，如 water(水), air(空氣), sugar(糖)。

🎵 5.抽象名詞，如 patience(耐心), disappointment(失望), love(愛)。

什麼時候用名詞？

1. 主詞得用名詞。例如：

🎵 <u>Karaoke</u> is popular in Taiwan.
卡拉 OK 在台灣很流行。

🎵 <u>Vegetables</u> are good for your health.
蔬菜對你的健康有益。

2. 所有格後面用名詞。例如：

🎵 Amy's <u>purse</u> was stolen.
愛咪的錢包被偷了。

🎵 The doctor didn't know the cause of his <u>illness</u>.
醫生不知道他的病因。

3. 受詞用名詞。例如：

🎵 I love this <u>novel</u>.
我喜歡這本小說。(短篇小說是 short story。)

🎵 They eat <u>rice</u> every day.
他們每天都吃米飯。

4. 介系詞後面用名詞。例如：

🎵 She is obsessed with <u>computer games</u>.
她迷上電腦遊戲。

🎵 He doesn't work for <u>Mr. Chen</u> anymore.
他不再為陳先生工作了。

5. 當主詞指的就是後面的詞，這個後面的詞叫做補語，補語要
   用名詞。

   ♪ I am a <u>college student</u>.
     我是大學生。

   ♪ We are <u>classmates</u>.
     我們是同班同學。

朗讀 CD 第 1 軌

互動光碟

1-1 生字 Vocabulary

elementary school	小學
retire	退休（retire, retired, retired）
grade	打分數（動詞）（grade, graded, graded）；分數（名詞）
step by step	一步一步，按步就班
community college	社區大學
pick	選，摘（pick, picked, picked）
course	課程
register	註冊（register, registered, registered）
driving school	駕駛訓練班
sign up	報名（sign, signed, signed）
driving lessons	駕駛課
sense of direction	方向感
turn someone's back to（a person）	轉身以背對著（某人）（turn, turned, turned）

朗讀 CD 第 2 軌

互動光碟

1-2 課文 Text

My mom is an[1] **elementary school** teacher. She has been teaching kids for almost 25 years[2]. This summer she will **retire**[3]. Now, besides[4] teaching students and **grading**[5] their homework and tests, she is planning her retirement **step by step**.

First, she visited the **community college** near our home. After **picking**[6] a few[7] interesting **courses**[8], she **registered**[9] right away. Then she found a **driving school** and **signed up**[10] for **driving lessons**[11]. When my dad found out, he laughed[12], "You don't have any **sense of direction**[13]—how can you drive a car?" "Wait and see!" said my mom, then **turned her back to**[14] him and walked away.

我的媽媽是位小學老師。她教小孩幾乎教了 25 年，今年暑假她會退休。現在除了教書和批改學生作業和考卷外，她正一步步計畫退休生活。

首先，她參觀了我們家附近的社區大學。選了一些有趣的課之後，她立刻註冊。接著她找到一家駕駛訓練班，報名上駕駛課。當爸爸發現時，他大笑：「妳一點方向感都沒有，妳怎麼可以開車？」媽媽說：「等著瞧！」接著就轉身走人。

朗讀 CD 第 3 軌

互動光碟

 1-4 解析 Language Focus

1. elementary school teacher(小學老師)是名詞,當作 my mom 的補語。elementary 字首發音是母音,所以 a 要改為 an。

2. 這句用的是現在完成進行式,因為作者的母親直到現在還在小學任教,因此這句可改寫為 This summer she will have been teaching for 25 years.,意思是今年夏天還沒到,而到今年夏天為止,她將在小學教了 25 年。

3. retire 是動詞。retired 是形容詞。retirement 是名詞。例如:

   🎵 She will retire in June.
   她將在六月退休。

   🎵 She is retired.
   她退休了。

   🎵 She finished a book during her retirement.
   她在退休期間完成了一本書。

4. besides 常和 except 及 beside 混淆。besides 是「除了……之外還有……」,與 in additon to 同義。except 是「除了……之外,其他所有都……」。beside 是介系詞,意思是「在……的旁邊」。

   🎵 Besides the piano, she plays the violin.(besides = in additon to)
   除了鋼琴,她還拉小提琴。(她會彈鋼琴,也會拉小提琴。)

   🎵 She likes all kands of novels except science fiction.
   = Except for science fiction, she likes all kinds of novels.
   除了科幻小說,其他所有的小說她都喜歡。(她不喜歡讀科幻小說。)

   🎵 Who is the girl sitting beside Peter?
   坐在彼得旁邊的女孩是誰?

5.　besides 在此當作介系詞，後面接名詞，所以 teach 和 grade 兩個動詞要改成動名詞 teaching 和 grading。grade 當名詞時意指「成績」，當動詞時是指「批改(考卷等)，打分數」。例如：

　　🎧　I hope I get a good grade.
　　　　我希望拿到好成績。

　　🎧　I will grade students' papers tonight.
　　　　今晚我會批改學生的報告。

　　此外，grade 也指「(從小學到高中一到十二)年級」。

　　🎧　He is in the sixth grade.
　　　　＝ He is a sixth-grader.
　　　　他小學六年級。

　　但大學的「年級」不用 grade 表示，説明如下：

　　🎧　I am a junior. 我大三。

　　大學各年級學生説法：

freshman	大一學生
sophomore	大二學生
junior	大三學生
senior	大四學生

6.　動詞 pick 在介系詞 after 後面，要改為動名詞 picking。

7.　little, a little; few, a few 常常容易混淆，請看説明及例句：

　　little(很少，形容不可數的名詞)

　　🎧　I have little free time to hang out with friends.
　　　　我很少有空跟朋友一起玩。

　　a little(一些些，形容不可數的名詞)

　　🎧　Besides studying, I have a little free time to hang out with friends.
　　　　除了讀書，我還有一些空閒時間跟朋友一起玩。

few（很少，形容可數的名詞）

　　🕮　Few people will vote for him.
　　　　很少有人會投票給他。

a few（一些些，形容可數的名詞）

　　🕮　A few people may vote for him.
　　　　一些人也許會投票給他。

8.　course（課程），teach courses（教課），take courses（修課）

　　🕮　How many courses are you taking this semester?
　　　　這學期你修幾門課？

　　🕮　How many courses are you teaching this semester?
　　　　這學期你教幾門課？

9.　register 動詞，registration 名詞，registered 形容詞。例句：

　　🕮　I failed to register for this course.
　　　　我沒有註冊（登記）到這門課。

　　🕮　Please show me your car registration number.
　　　　請給我看你的汽車註冊號碼（牌照號碼）。

　　🕮　Registered mail usually costs more.
　　　　掛號信通常較貴。（mail 是不可數名詞，不加s；letter 則是可數名詞，可加 s。）

10.　sign up 報名

　　🕮　She signed up for evening classes.
　　　　她報名夜間部的課。

　　🕮　He signed his name on the form.
　　　　他在表格上簽名。

11.　一般人到 driving school（駕駛訓練班）報名 driving lessons（駕駛課程），希望拿到 driver's license（汽車駕照）。

12. laugh 笑，大笑（動詞）laughter 笑聲（名詞）

13. direct 指點（動詞），director 導演（名詞），direction 方向（名詞）

14. turn one's back to someone 指「轉身走人」，但片語 turn one's back on someone 則指「拒絕幫助某人」。

1-5-1 選選看

1. My mom is interested in _____.

    (a) drive　(b) driving　(c) drove

2. His _____ in hip hop（嘻哈）music didn't last very long（不持久）.

    (a) interesting　(b) interested　(c) interest

3. During his _____, he has traveled abroad（國外旅遊）many times.

    (a) retire　(b) retired　(c) retirement

4. What are your _____ for the next three years?

    (a) plans　(b) planning　(c) planned

5. Your car _____ has expired（已經過期）.

    (a) register　(b) registration　(c) registered

6. Cram schools（補習班）teach students how to get high _____ on entrance exams.

    (a) grading　(b) graded　(c) grades

7. Besides _____ baseball, they also like to go bowling（打保齡球）.

    (a) playing　(b) play　(c) played

8. A stranger asked me for _____（問路）.

    (a) directions　(b) directing　(c) direct

9. Their _____（笑聲）filled the classroom.

    (a) laughing　(b) laugh　(c) laughter

10. Who is the _____（導演）of that movie?

　　(a) direct　(b) director　(c) directing

11. She is crazy about _____ sports cars.

　　(a) drive　(b) driver　(c) driving

12. They are _____ English teachers.

　　(a) retired　(b) retiring　(c) retire

13. _____ your name at the end of this form is the first step（第一步）for registering.

　　(a) Sign　(b) Signed　(c) Signing

14. Mary's _____ her back to her husband made him angry.

　　(a) turn　(b) turning　(c) turned

15. My _____ at a community college is not just for money.

　　(a) teaching　(b) teach　(c) taught

1-5-2 填填看

few,　a few,　little,　a little

1. There is _____ food left. I need to cook some more.

2. Only _____ people can do this job.

3. Her directions are _____ help to us. I think we can finish it with out her.

4. There were _____ mistakes（幾乎沒有錯誤）in her writing.

5. I need to put _____ more sugar in my coffee.

6. Only _____ voters（選民）believed what he had said.

7. My sister had done most of the work. There was _____ I could do to help.

8. Could you spare me _____ minutes（給我幾分鐘）?

9. Could you lend me _____ dollars?

10. There is _____ I can do about this.

11. May I have _____ more ice cream?

12. He got drunk from drinking _____ beer.

13. I can't finish the work in time with so _____ time.

14. What your pets（寵物）need is _____ love and attention.

15. There are not many students here. Just _____.

1-5-3 問答

1.　Is the writer's mom an elementary school teacher?

　　例：Yes, she is. _____

2.　Will she still be a teacher next year?

　　_____

3.　Is she retired now?

　　_____

4.　How long has she been teaching?

　　_____

5.　Who are her students? Elementary school students, junior high school students, high school students, or college students?

　　_____

6.　What is she doing besides teaching students and grading their homework?

　　_____

7.　When she was planning her retirement, what did she do first?

　　_____

8.　After picking interesting courses, what did she do next?

　　_____

9. After finding a driving school, what did she do next?

_____

10. Why did she want to take driving lessons?(提示：driver's license)

_____

11. Why did the writer's dad laugh at his mom?

He laughed because _____

12. What was his mom's reaction(反應)to his dad's words？

His mom _____

1-5-4 英文該怎麼寫？

1. 我一步步學英文。

_____

2. 我的父母已經退休了。

_____

3. 我每年夏天都在社區大學修課。

_____

4. 他退休後在社區大學教數學(math)。（After he retired,...）

_____

5. 你上過駕訓課沒有？（Have you taken...）

_____

6. 我的表弟妹都是小學生。

_____

7. 我的堂弟是小學三年級學生。

_____

8. 你家附近有沒有駕駛訓練學校？(Is there...)

   _____

9. 這封信要不要掛號？(...need to be...)

   _____

10. 你昨天報名烹飪班了嗎？(...the cooking class?)

   _____

答案請見 pp. 159-160

第二課 Unit 2

詞類變化——動名詞

互動光碟

動名詞(動詞原形＋ing)，顧名思義，就是名詞化之後的動詞。動詞名詞化之後，本身雖有動作的意涵，不過功能上卻當作名詞使用。動詞為什麼要名詞化呢？因為一個動詞在句子中不再具備動詞的功能，轉而擔任名詞的角色，這時候的動詞叫做動名詞，後面要加 ing。

大部分的動詞加 ing 的過程非常簡單，只要直接在動詞後面加 ing 即可，如 studying、working、sleeping 等，不過有的動詞在加 ing 的過程中本身要做一些變動，請看下面一些特殊的狀況：

I.　shop、swim 和 sit 這些只有一個音節的動詞，它們最後一個字母 p、m 和 t 前面的母音都是短母音，加 ing 時要重複最後一個字母：shopping、swimming 和 sitting。

*　注意：visit 雖有短母音，但有兩個音節 vi sit，所以加 ing 時不必重複最後一個字母，直接加 ing，寫成 visiting 即可。

*　注意：buy 最後字母 y 前面的 u 看起來是母音，但發音卻是長母音，所以加 ing 時，不能重複 y，直接加 ing，寫成 buying 即可。

II.　admit、prefer 和 forget 有兩個音節，又都是短母音，因為重音在第二音節，加 ing 時要重複最後一個字母：admitting、preferring 和 forgetting。

*　注意：edit、visit 有兩個音節，也都是短母音，不過因為重音在第一音節，加 ing 時不必重複最後一個字母：editing、visiting。

III.　通常最後一個字母是 y 的動詞，如 play、enjoy、study 和 worry 等可以直接加 ing，寫成 playing、enjoying、studying 和 worrying。

IV.　take、make、use、smile、exercise 和 hope 這些動詞的最後一

個字母是 e，加 ing 時，記得要把 e 去掉，再加 ing：taking、making、using、smiling、exercising 和 hoping。

V.　die 和 tie 等字尾是 ie 的動詞，加 ing 時要把 ie 去掉，變成 y，再加 ing：dying 和 tying。

什麼時候動詞要名詞化變成動名詞呢？請看下面說明：

I.　動詞當主詞時要轉成動名詞，例如：

　　🐦 Collecting stuffed animals is my hobby.
　　　收集填充玩具是我的嗜好。

＊　動詞當主詞時也可以用不定詞(to+V)取代動名詞，此句也可以寫成：

　　🐦 To collect stuffed animals is my hobby.

II.　主詞指的就是某種動作行為時，動詞要轉成動名詞。(my hobby = collecting...)，例如：

　　🐦 My hobby is collecting stuffed animals.
　　　我的嗜好是收集填充玩具。

III.　動詞放在介系詞後面要轉成動名詞。(見中級本第16課16-4)，例如：

　　🐦 She insists on calling him tonight.
　　　她堅持今晚打電話給他。

IV.　所有格後面的動詞要轉成動名詞，例如：

　　🐦 Peter's cheating led to his failing this course.
　　　彼得作弊導致他這門課不及格。

♪ His <u>laughing</u> at me made me angry.
他嘲笑我這件事讓我生氣。

V. 有些動詞後面可接不定詞(to+動詞原形)或動名詞(動詞原形＋ing)。(見中級本第 9 課)例如：

♪ I love <u>swimming</u>. 或 I love to swim.
我愛游泳。

♪ He hates <u>exercising</u>. 或 He hates to exercise.
他討厭做運動。

♪ She continues <u>working</u> on this project. 或 She continues to work on this project.
她繼續做這個計畫。

有些動詞(如 finish, enjoy, avoid, mind, complete, practice, spend)後面一定要接動名詞，例如：

♪ I finally finished <u>writing</u> this report.
我終於寫完了這份報告。

♪ He enjoys <u>sending</u> text messages to his friends.
他喜歡傳簡訊給朋友。

♪ She avoids <u>meeting</u> her ex-boyfriend.
她避免跟前任男友碰面。

♪ They keep <u>walking</u>.
他們一直走著。

♪ He spent two hours <u>walking</u> his dog.
他花了兩小時遛狗。

VI. 有些慣用語的後面要接動名詞，例如：

🖐 <u>Thank you for helping</u> me finish this project.
謝謝你幫我完成這個計畫。

🖐 We <u>are used to taking</u> a cold shower in the winter.
我們習慣冬天洗冷水澡。

🖐 I <u>am looking forward to meeting</u> you.
我期待與您相見。（商業書信文末常見的一句客套話。）

🖐 <u>How about seeing</u> a movie this afternoon?
今天下午看場電影如何？

🖐 I <u>can't help crying</u>.
我忍不住哭了。

🖐 I <u>had trouble finding</u> my way back home.
我找不到回家的路。

🖐 We <u>had fun staying</u> here.
我們待在這裡很開心。

互動光碟

2-1 生字 Vocabulary

trick	伎倆
discourage	勸阻（discourage, discouraged, discouraged）
strengthen	加強（strengthen, strengthened, strengthened）
continue	繼續（continue, continued, continued）
be different from	與……不同（be, was/were, been）
used to	過去習慣於……（現在已不再做）
civil servant	公務員
get up/wake up	起床（get, got, got/gotten; wake, waked, waked）
rush to	匆忙去（rush, rushed, rushed）
have a bite to eat	隨便吃（have, had, had）
roadside stand	路邊攤
tend to	易於，傾向於，往往（tend, tended, tended）
dress down	隨便穿（dress, dressed, dressed）

be used to	習慣於(be, was/were, been)
tank top	汗衫背心
shorts	短褲
flip-flops	拖鞋(夾腳拖鞋)
talk show	談話性節目
pastime	休閒活動

朗讀 CD 第 5 軌

互動光碟

2-2 課文 Text

Discouraging[1] Mom is Dad's old **trick**[2]. However, this time his words didn't **discourage** her. Instead, they **strengthened**[3] her will to **continue** learning and trying[4] new things. She plans[5] on having a life of her own[6], a life far **different from** her retired husband's[7].

My dad has been retired for a year already. He **used to**[8] be a **civil servant**. Now he is happy because he doesn't have to **get up** early and **rush to** get to the office on time. Usually he gets up at nine o'clock in the morning. If he doesn't make breakfast for himself, he **has a bite to eat**[9] at a **roadside stand**. Since[10] he spends[11] most of his time staying home, he tends to **dress down**[12]. He **is used to** wearing a **tank top**, **shorts**, and **flip-flops** at home. Watching **talk shows** on TV is his favorite **pastime**.

2-3 課文翻譯

　　勸阻媽媽是爸爸的一慣伎倆。不過這次他的話卻沒有打消媽媽的想法，反倒加強了她繼續學習和嘗試新東西的意念。她計畫過自己的生活，一個與她退了休的先生迥然不同的生活。

　　爸爸退休已經一年了，他過去是公務員。現在他很高興不必早起並趕著準時去上班。通常他早上九點才醒來。如果他不自己做早餐的話，他就隨便在路邊攤吃。因為他都待在家裡，他往往穿著隨便。在家他習慣穿著一件汗衫、一條短褲和一雙拖鞋，他最喜歡的活動就是看電視上的談話性節目。

朗讀 CD 第 6 軌

2-4 解析 Language Focus

 互動光碟

1. discourage 是動詞，discouragement 是名詞，discouraging 是形容詞，discouraged 是過去分詞（作形容詞用時，可指「氣餒的，洩氣的」）（見中級本16課）。

　　🎵 He tried to <u>discourage</u> me from taking this part-time job at the convenience store.
　　他試著勸我不要接這份在便利商店打工的工作。

　　🎵 I won't listen to his <u>discouragement</u> though.
　　不過我不會聽他勸阻的話。

　　🎵 His <u>discouraging</u> words made me angry.
　　他勸阻的話令我生氣。

　　🎵 I won't let myself be <u>discouraged</u> by him.
　　我不會讓自己被他勸阻的。

2. trick 是名詞也是動詞，名詞是「伎倆」，當動詞則是「作弄」。

　　🎵 He likes to <u>play tricks on</u> people.
　　他喜歡戲弄人。

　　🎵 She showed me many card <u>tricks</u>.
　　她表演許多撲克牌的把戲給我看

　　🎵 He often <u>tricks</u> people and makes them upset.
　　他常常作弄別人，讓人不開心。

3. strength 優點（名詞），strengthen 加強（動詞），strong 堅強的，強壯的（形容詞）。

　　🎵 She knows her <u>strengths</u> and weaknesses very well.
　　她非常了解自己的優點和缺點。

ᕄ The government is trying to <u>strengthen</u> the banking system.
政府正試著強化銀行系統。

ᕄ Only a person with a <u>strong</u> will can survive.
只有擁有堅強意志力的人才能存活。

4. continue 後面可以接動名詞(V+ing)，也可以接不定詞(to+V)

5. plan on <u>doing</u> something = plan <u>to do</u> something

6. ...of...（……的）例如：

 my book = the book of mine 我的書

 his decision = the decision of his 他自己的決定

7. her husband's = her husband's life

8. used to（過去的習慣）和 be used to（習慣一種狀況到了可以接受的地步）很容易混淆。請看例句：

 a. used to ＋ 動詞原形

 ᕄ He <u>used to</u> ride his scooter to school, but now he rides his bike.
他過去騎摩托車上學，但是他現在騎腳踏車。

 ᕄ A: <u>Did</u> you <u>use to</u> swim every day?
你過去每天游泳嗎？

 ᕄ B: Yes, I <u>used to</u> swim every day, but now I don't because I hurt my leg.
是的，我過去每天游泳，不過現在不游，因為我的腳受了傷。

 b. be used to ＋ 動名詞(V+ing)或名詞　習慣做……的，習慣某事物

 ᕄ My sister is used to <u>getting</u> up early for school.
我的姊姊習慣早起上學。

 ᕄ Are you used to <u>spicy food</u>?
你習慣吃重口味的菜嗎？（如川菜很 spicy，因為放很多 spices「香料」）

9. has a bite to eat 隨便吃點東西；dine out 出去吃（到餐館用餐）

10. since 有兩個常用的意思：1.自從（參看中級本 12-4），2. 因為，既然

   ♪ We have been good friends <u>since</u> we <u>were</u> in middle school.
   我們自國中起就是好朋友了。

* 注意 since 的後面是過去式，前面用現在完成式。）

   ♪ <u>Since</u> I put on weight easily, I always stay away from fast food.
   因為我很容易變胖，我總是遠離速食。

11. 動詞 spend 後面加動詞，動詞要加 ing。例如：

   ♪ I <u>spent</u> the whole night <u>finishing</u> this project.
   我花了一整晚才完成這個計畫。

12. dress down 穿著隨便；dress up 穿著正式。例如參加派對前你不確定派對的性質，可以先問主人：

   ♪ Is it a formal party or informal party?
   是正式還是非正式的派對呢？

不知穿什麼衣服合適，可以問主人：

   ♪ Shonld I dress up or dress down?
   我該盛裝還是一般打扮就好？

2-5-1 選選看

1.　He spends time_____ science fiction(科幻小說).

　　(a)read　(b)to read　(c)reading

2.　I am looking forward to _____ you.

　　(a)meeting　(b)meet　(c)met

3.　We are used to _____ clothes at the thrift shop(二手店).

　　(a)buy　(b)buying　(c)bought

4.　I _____ to find a job at the convenience store.

　　(a)plans　(b)planning　(c)planned

5.　She finally quit _____ computer games last semester(上學期).

　　(a)plays　(b)to play　(c)playing

6.　The baby kept _____ for an hour.

　　(a)crying　(b)to cry　(c)cried

7.　_____ is good exercise.

　　(a)Swim　(b)Swam　(c)Swimming

8.　I used to _____ my dog in the morning when I was young.

　　(a)walking　(b)walked　(c)walk

9.　You should avoid _____ out in the evening.

　　(a)go　(b)going　(c)to go

10.　The teacher insisted on _____ us a test tomorrow.

　　(a)give　(b)to give　(c)giving

11. She is excited about _____ him tonight.

    (a)to meet   (b)meet   (c)meeting

12. The doctor is planning on _____ abroad（出國進修）.

    (a)to study   (b)studying   (c)studied

13. How about _____ lunch with me?

    (a)had   (b)having   (c)have

14. Mary began to _____ the guitar again.

    (a)play   (b)playing   (c)played

15. Thank you for _____ my son English.

    (a)teaching   (b)teach   (c)taught

2-5-2 填填看

V+ing 或是 to+V（有些題目兩個答案都可以）

1. _____ (go)to parties is fun.

2. He wants _____ (swim).

3. She is afraid of _____ (go)by plane（搭飛機）.

4. I can't help _____ (write)a letter to her.

5. She decided _____ (forgive)him.

6. He spent some time _____ (read)the novel.

7. My sister keeps _____ (lend)money to him.

8. We are looking forward to _____ (win)this game.

9. They had problems _____ (tell)her the truth.

10. _____ (sell)this old house is not easy.

11. I enjoy _____ (cook).

12. It is easy _____ (drive)a car.

13. I used _____ (sleep) late. (我過去一向晚起。)

14. I am used to _____ (sleep) late. (我一直習慣晚起。)

15. Are you planning on _____ (go) to the party?

2-5-3 問答

1. Did the author's (作者的) dad's words discourage his mom?

   例：No, they didn't. _____

2. Will his mom continue learning new things?

   _____

3. Is his dad retired?

   _____

4. How long has his dad been retired?

   _____

5. What did his dad use to do?

   _____

6. Is his dad happy with his life after retiring?

   _____

7. When does his dad usually get up?

   _____

8. Where does his dad eat breakfast?

   _____

9. What kind of shoes does his dad wear at home?

   _____

10. What is his dad's favorite pastime?

    _____

2-5-4 改錯

1.　He is tieing his shoe laces（鞋帶）.

2.　She goes swiming almost every day.

3.　They laughing at her upset her.

4.　I like to sending text messages to my friends.

5.　She is not used to go out at night.

6.　Play badminton is her favorite activity.

7.　I spent all my energy（花了我所有的精力）to do the project.

8.　We couldn't help to cry when we heard this bad news.

9.　We will never let ourselves be discouraging.

10.　They tried to strong their belief in God.

2-5-5 英文該怎麼寫？

1.　我最喜歡的休閒活動是讀英文小說。

　　_____

2.　我的爸爸習慣早起。

　　_____

3.　不要打消我學英文（的念頭）。（Don't discourage me from...）

　　_____

4.　我過去一直在社區大學教英文。

　　_____

5.　我的興趣跟他的（his）很不同。

　　_____

6.　我的姊姊已經退休三年了。

　　_____

7. 他正在路邊攤隨便吃些東西。

    _____

8. 她每天6點起床。

    _____

9. 收集漫畫書(comic books)是我的嗜好。

    _____

10. 他正穿著夾腳拖鞋在路邊攤吃東西。(He is wearing...)

    _____

答案請見 pp. 160-161

第三課 Unit 3

動詞──三態變化

互動光碟

　　說完了動名詞,我們再回頭來看動詞。動詞是一個句子最主要的部分,沒有動詞,句子不算完整。動詞分為 be 動詞(如 am, is, are 等)和一般動詞(如 have, do, take, play 等)。在一個句子中,動詞得和前面主詞一致(這些我們在初級本都學過了),例如 I 後面的 be 動詞要用 am,We 後面的 be 動詞要用 are,還有第三人稱動詞後面要加 s 等等……請看下面例句:

🎧 I <u>am</u> at home right now.
　　我現在在家。

🎧 She <u>has</u> a headache.
　　她頭痛。

🎧 He often <u>teaches</u> his daughter math.
　　他常教女兒數學。

　　一般動詞又可以分為<u>及物動詞</u>和<u>不及物動詞</u>,及物動詞的後面接受詞,不及物動詞後面不可接受詞如:

🎧 She <u>wrote a novel</u> last year.
　　她去年寫了一本小說。(wrote 是及物動詞,a novel 是它的受詞。)

有的及物動詞有兩個受詞,如:

🎧 He <u>gave me a book</u>.
　　他給了我一本書。(gave 是及物動詞,me 和 a book 都是它的受詞。)

🎧 He <u>fell</u> down yesterday.
　　昨天他跌倒了。(fell 是不及物動詞,後面沒有受詞。)

⑨ Birds fly.

　　鳥飛。(fly 是不及物動詞，後面沒有受詞，句子依然完整。)

　　每個動詞都有三態變化，有的動詞變化很規則，只要加 ed 就好了，如：

⑨ play, play<u>ed</u>, play<u>ed</u>

⑨ walk, walk<u>ed</u>, walk<u>ed</u>

⑨ talk, talk<u>ed</u>, talk<u>ed</u>

　　但也有很多動詞的三態變化不依照加 ed 的規則，不過這些不規則動詞的三態變化，隱約可以分出下面幾種規則：

⑨ 1. 三態同形：如 quit, quit, quit

　　　　　　　　　cost, cost, cost

⑨ 2. 二、三態相同：如 bring, brought, brought

　　　　　　　　　feel, felt, felt

⑨ 3. 一、三態相同：如 come, came, come

　　　　　　　　　run, ran, run

⑨ 4. 一、二、三態各不同：如 bite, bit, bitten

　　　　　　　　　　choose, chose, chosen

　　為什麼動詞要有三態變化？動詞三種變化各自的作用何在？我們現在將動詞三態變化的用法分別解釋，並舉例詳加說明：

I. 動詞第一態變化：動詞原形

1. 助動詞(will, would, shall, should, can, could, may, might, do, did...)後面要用動詞原形(請看中級本19課)。例如：

He <u>will</u> <u>bring</u> you some food.
他會帶一些吃的東西給你。

I <u>can</u> <u>speak</u> some English now.
我現在會說些英文了。

<u>Did</u> you <u>watch</u> TV last night?
你昨晚看電視了嗎？

<u>Should</u> I <u>meet</u> her tonight or not?
我今晚應不應該見她？

You <u>must</u> <u>see</u> her tonight.
你今晚一定得見她。

2. 不定詞 to 後面要接動詞原形。例如：

I want to <u>have</u> a dog.
我想要一隻狗。

He decided to <u>go</u> back to school.
他決定回學校（讀書）。

* 注意第二課提到的兩個慣用語，雖以 to 結尾，卻不接動詞原形的例子：

I <u>am used to</u> getting up early.
我習慣早起。

I am looking forward <u>to</u> seeing you.
我期待見到你。

3. 命令句要用動詞原形。例如：

<u>Stand</u> up.
站起來。

🔊 Turn around.
轉個身。

🔊 Don't touch that dog!
別碰那隻狗！

4. 習慣用語後面用動詞原形。例如：

🔊 You had better see a doctor right now.
你最好現在就去看醫生。

🔊 I would rather stay at home than see a movie.
我寧願待在家裡也不願去看電影。

5. have、let 和 make 等使役動詞後面接原形動詞。例如：

🔊 She had me do extra work.
她要我做額外的工作。

🔊 He made me feel unhappy.
他讓我覺得不快樂。

🔊 Let's eat some ice cream.
我們吃些冰淇淋吧。（let's = let us）

6. 感官動詞 see, look at, watch, listen, hear, listen to, taste, smell, feel 後面接原形動詞。

🔊 I watched him slide down.
我看他滑下去。

🔊 I heard the baby cry last night.
我昨晚聽到嬰兒哭。

🕭 I could <u>feel</u> my heart <u>sink</u>.

我可以感覺到我的心往下沈。

* 主詞＋感官動詞＋受詞＋動詞原形 → 強調事實

🕭 We heard birds sing.

我們聽到鳥叫聲。

* 主詞＋感官動詞＋受詞＋（動詞＋V-ing）→ 強調動作正在進行

🕭 We heard birds singing.

我們聽到鳥兒正在叫。

7. 現在式用動詞原形，不過動詞遇到第三人稱時要加 s。例如：

🕭 <u>She</u> always <u>takes</u> her dog to school.

她總是帶著狗去上學。

🕭 <u>The dog</u> <u>runs</u> out every night.

這隻狗每晚都跑出去。

🕭 <u>We</u> <u>take</u> a trip to Hualian every summer.

每年夏天我們都去花蓮旅行。

II. 動詞第二態變化：過去式（請看初級本第 15 課）

看到以下過去的時段，要用過去式：

1. 某個特定過去的時間：at 7:30 this morning, at 5 o'clock this afternoon
   例如：

   🕭 <u>At 2:15 I</u> <u>went</u> to see a movie.

   兩點十五分時我去看了一場電影。

2. ……之前：three days ago, two hours ago 例如：

   🕭 <u>I</u> <u>met</u> him <u>a few minutes ago</u>.

   幾分鐘之前我遇到了他。

3.　yesterday 昨天 或 the day before yesterday 前天，例如：

　　🎧　I <u>didn't go</u> to school <u>the day before yesterday</u>.
　　　　前天我沒去上學。

4.　上……: last week 上星期、last month 上個月、last year 去年、last
　　August 去年八月、last Thursday 上星期四 例如：

　　🎧　He <u>showed</u> me a beautiful stone last week.
　　　　他上星期給我看一塊美麗的石頭。

5.　on 某一日、in 某一年：<u>on</u> December 23rd, 1991、<u>in</u> 1545 例如：

　　🎧　In 1993 she left home. 她於1993年離家。

6.　當……時候：When I was 5 years old...例如：

　　🎧　When I was young, I <u>played</u> video games every night.
　　　　我小時候每晚都打電動。

III. 動詞第三態變化：過去分詞

1. 現在完成式和過去完成式用 have/has/had＋過去分詞(請看中級本
　　11課和13課)例如：

　　🎧　He <u>has seen</u> three movies this week.(see, saw, seen)
　　　　這星期他已經看了三部電影。

　　🎧　I <u>had</u> never <u>seen</u> such a beautiful beach before I went to
　　　　Kenting.(see, saw, seen)
　　　　我去墾丁之前從來沒有看過這麼美的海灘。

2. 表示被動時，用 be 動詞＋過去分詞(請看中級本第15課)例如：

　　🎧　He <u>was taken</u> to the hospital by an ambulance.(take, took, taken)
　　　　他被救護車載去醫院。

朗讀 CD 第 7 軌

互動光碟

3-1 生字 Vocabulary

as	當……
essay	作文
study	書房(名詞)
hear	聽到(hear, heard, heard)
hold	拿著(hold, held, held)
soymilk	豆漿
carry	帶回(carry, carried, carried)
imagine	想像(imagine, imagined, imagined)
the rest of	其餘的,剩下來的
sit	坐(sit, sat, sat)
comfortable	舒服的
couch	長沙發椅
smell	聞到(smell, smelled, smelled)
know	知道(know, knew, known)
tell	告訴(tell, told, told)
quit	戒、停止(quit, quit, quit)

stubborn	固執的
bother	煩惱、麻煩（bother, bothered, bothered）
nag	囉唆（nag, nagged, nagged）
enjoy	享受（enjoy, enjoyed, enjoyed）
cigarette	香菸
strange	奇怪的
fight	爭吵（名詞）

朗讀 CD 第 8 軌

互動光碟

3-2 課文 Text

　　As I was working[1] on an **essay** in my **study**, I **heard**[2] my dad come home. Through the window, I saw[3] him **holding** a cup of **soymilk** in his hand and **carrying** the newspaper on his head. You can **imagine**[4] how funny he looked! For **the rest of** the morning, he **sat** on a **comfortable couch**[5] reading the newspaper.

　　Then I **smelled** smoke[6]. I **knew** it was coming from my dad. He was smoking in the living room! My mom has **told**[7] him many times to **quit**[8] smoking. But being[9] a **stubborn** person, he has never even **bothered**[10] to try. Without his wife around **nagging**[11] him, he could **enjoy** his free time reading the paper[12] and smoking **cigarettes**. However, when my mom comes home and smells something **strange**, they are going to have a big **fight**[13].

3-3 課文翻譯

　　當我正在書房寫作文時，我聽到爸爸回家了。從窗口看出去，我看到他手裡拿著豆漿，頭頂著報紙。你可以想像他看起來多滑稽！早晨其餘時間，他就坐在舒適的長沙發上，讀著報紙。

　　接著我聞到了菸味。知道菸味是從爸爸傳那裡來的。他居然還在客廳抽菸！媽媽曾經多次叫他戒菸。但這位固執的老爸，連試都不想試。沒有太太在一旁碎碎唸，他可以好好享受這段自由時間，邊看報、邊抽菸。但只要媽媽回來聞到奇怪的味道，他們準會大吵一架。

朗讀 CD 第 9 軌

互動光碟

3-4 解析 Language Focus

1. 過去一件事情正在進行（寫作文），另外一件事（我聽到……）同時發生了，這時前者用過去進行式，後者用過去式。例如：

   ✎ As I was taking a shower, he called me.
   我正在洗澡時，他打電話給我。

2. hear 是感官動詞，後面接原形動詞或動名詞。例如：

   ✎ I heard him play the piano.
   我聽到他彈鋼琴。（彈琴的動作已結束）

   ✎ I heard him playing the piano.
   我聽到他正在彈鋼琴。（彈琴的動作正在進行）

3. see 也是感官動詞，後面接原形動詞或動名詞。例如：

   ✎ I saw him hand a cup of soymilk to his girlfriend.
   我看他拿了一杯豆漿遞給女朋友。

   ✎ I saw him holding a cup of soymilk.
   我看他正拿著一杯豆漿。

4. imagine 想像（動詞），imagination 想像力（名詞）

   ✎ I imagined myself flying in the sky.
   我想像自己在天上飛。

   ✎ He lacks imagination.
   他缺少想像力。

5. couch 長沙發，許多人喜歡坐在沙發上看電視，久而久之，就變得愈來愈胖，被譏為 couch potato。

6. smoke 可以當名詞──「煙」，也可以當動詞──「抽菸」，smoked 是形容詞，指「煙燻的」，例如：

   ◊ <u>Smoke</u> is coming out of that house.
     煙正從那間屋子出來。

   ◊ He <u>is smoking</u> a cigarette.
     他正在抽菸。

   ◊ I like <u>smoked</u> chicken sandwiches.
     我喜歡燻雞三明治

7. 媽媽已經跟他說(tell, told, told)了好幾次，用「現在完成式」。

8. quit 跟 enjoy、avoid、spend 一樣，後面接的動詞要用動名詞，如

   ◊ I <u>quit</u> <u>playing</u> computer games.
     我不打電玩了。

   ◊ I <u>quit</u> <u>drinking</u>.
     我戒酒了。

9. He is a stubborn person. He has never bothered to try.

兩個句子的主詞都是 he，連成一個句子時，前面的 he 可以省略，is 改為動名詞 being，即 Being a stubborn person, he has never bothered to try. 請看下面另外一個例子，(1)兩句的主詞都是 she，可以將動詞 had 改為動名詞 having，合為一句(2)：

   ◊ (1)She <u>had</u> worked on the project all day. She felt very tired.

   ◊ (2)<u>Having</u> worked on the project all day, she felt very tired.
     做了一整天計畫，她感到非常疲累。

10. He has never even bothered to try. 他連試都不想試。

   ◊ He has never even bothered to write. 他連寫都不想寫。

   ◊ I won't bother him. 我不會麻煩他。

🎧　Don't bother.
不用麻煩。

🎧　Why bother?
何必呢？

11.　nag（動詞），nagging（名詞）

🎧　He <u>nags</u> me all the time.
他一直跟我囉唆個沒完。

🎧　His endless <u>nagging</u> is almost driving her crazy.
他無止盡的囉唆幾乎讓她發瘋。

12.　paper = newspaper 報紙（可數），paper 論文、報告（可數），paper 紙張（不可數）

13.　fight 搏鬥，戰鬥（名詞），fight 與……作戰（動詞）（fight, fought, fought）

🎧　After a long fight with cancer, she passed away.
長期抗癌後，她去世了。

🎧　He is fighting poverty.
他正在跟貧窮作戰。

3-5-1 選選看

1.　You must _____ the piano right now.

　　(a) to play　(b) play　(c) played

2.　Did he _____ you the book?

　　(a) gives　(b) giving　(c) give

3.　Have you _____ a smoked chicken sandwich before?

　　(a) have　(b) had　(c) has

4.　My dad _____ me to cut my hair.

　　(a) nagging　(b) nagged　(c) nag

5.　Stop _____.

　　(a) smoking　(b) smoked　(c) smoke

6.　Have you ever _____ with your brother?

　　(a) fight　(b) fighting　(c) fought

7.　She_____ me a bottle of soymilk this morning.

　　(a) bring　(b) brought　(c) brings

8.　After talking to me, she _____.

　　(a) disappears　(b) disappeared　(c) disappear.

9.　May I _____ here for a while?

　　(a) sitting　(b) sits　(c) sit

10.　The boy _____ very fast.

　　(a) run　(b) running　(c) runs

11. Has she _____ you her dog?

    (a) shown   (b) shows   (c) showed

12. I heard her _____ the violin.

    (a) plays   (b) playing   (c) played

13. She would rather _____ here than walk in the park.

    (a) sits   (b) sitting   (c) sit

14. He saw her _____ a new bag.

    (a) carrying   (b) carried   (c) carries

15. He has not even _____ to look up

    (a) bothered   (b) bothers   (c) bother

3-5-2 填填看

1. My dad used to _____ (smoke), but he has _____ (quit).

2. Her picture was _____ (see) by many people.

3. She is always being _____ (nag) by her elder sister.

4. This sofa has never been _____ (sit) on by anyone.

5. We have _____ (know) him for 10 years.

6. We have _____ (know) him since he was a little boy.

7. Did you _____ (smell) anything?

8. They just _____ (hear) a strange sound.

9. They _____ (come) home a few minutes ago.

10. He has _____ (drink) a bottle of soymilk.

11. How long have you _____ (work) on this project?

12. We _____ (sit) on the couch and fell asleep.

13. I _____ (feel) very bored last night.

14. He _____（fall）when he was having a heart attack.

15. Have you _____（read）this shocking news?

3-5-3 問答

1. When the writer was working on an essay, what did he hear?

   He heard _____.

2. Through the window, what did the writer see?

   He saw _____.

3. What was his dad doing when he sat on the couch?

   He _____.

4. What did the writer smell?

   He _____.

5. Where was his dad smoking?

   He _____.

6. Who has told his dad to quit smoking?

   _____.

7. Is the writer's dad a stubborn person?

   _____.

8. Has his dad ever tried to quit smoking?

   _____.

9. Who usually nags his dad when his dad is smoking?

   _____.

10. When his mom smells smoke what will happen?

    They _____.

3-5-4 改錯

1. He is always bother me when I am working on my essays.

2. We must to take a trip to Korea（韓國）together.

3. I knows him since he was a little boy.

4. This book was writing by a famous author.

5. She has bring many books home.

6. I heard the baby cried last night.

7. Last night she was show me a beautiful picture.

8. Could you held this for me for a minute?

9. She is often teach her daughter math.

10. This movie was not chose by me.

3-5-5 英文該怎麼寫？

1. 當我正在看電視時，我聽到一個奇怪的聲音。（As I was...）

   _____

2. 從窗子看出去，我看到一個小孩正在跑。（Through...）

   _____

3. 他總是坐在那張舒服的長沙發上聽音樂。（He always sits...）

   _____

4. 我聞到（smell）奇怪的味道。

   _____

5. 他今天早上買了三瓶（bottles）豆漿。

   _____

6. 我不習慣（be used to）抽菸。

   _____

7. 這對夫妻已經吵了30年了。(This couple...)

   _____

8. 她的先生是個固執的人。(Her husband...)

   _____

9. 我的姊姊喜歡在我寫作文時唸我。(When I am working on...)

   _____

10. 我跟他們說了好多次要停止(quit)吵架。(I've told...)

    _____

答案請見 pp. 161-163

第四課 Unit 4

動詞──動詞片語

互動光碟

　　動詞片語是一個動詞加上一個介系詞後，產生與原來動詞完全不同意思的組合。例如：I have to <u>pick</u> <u>up</u> my son.（我必須去接我兒子了。）pick up（接人）與 pick（摘）的意思完全不同，pick up 即動詞片語。

　　動詞片語 pick up 後面有受詞 my son，但並不是每個動詞片語後面都必須接受詞。動詞片語後面可以接受詞，也可以不接受詞，如：

> 　He will <u>show</u> <u>up</u> soon.（show up 後面沒有受詞。）
> 　他很快會出現。

> 　I have to <u>look</u> <u>after</u> <u>my mom</u>.（my mom 是 look after 的受詞。）
> 　我必須照顧我的母親。

I. 當動詞片語的受詞為「代名詞」時，受詞須放在動詞片語的動詞和介系詞之間（動詞＋受詞＋介系詞），如：

> 　You have to <u>do</u> <u>it</u> <u>over</u>. 你必須將它重做一遍。

＊　注意：當動詞片語的受詞為「一般名詞」時，受詞的位置放在動詞片語之間或之後（動詞＋受詞＋介系詞；動詞＋介系詞＋受詞），如 III 的說明。

II. 有的動詞必須和介系詞連在一起用（動詞＋介系詞＋受詞），如：

> 　I <u>ran</u> <u>into</u> my teacher in the park. 我在公園裡碰到老師。

III. 有的動詞和介系詞則可以分開，也可以不必分開來用。

> 　<u>Turn</u> <u>off</u> the light please.
> 　= <u>Turn</u> the light <u>off</u> please.
> 　請關燈。

IV. 有的動詞片語由三個字組成，受詞一律接在動詞片語之後，如：

- ∮ catch up with 追上

  You go first. I will catch up with you later.

  你先走。我待會兒再跟你會合。

- ∮ drop out of 退學

  He dropped out of school to work full-time.

  他退學以便全職工作。

- ∮ get rid of 除掉

  They tried to get rid of the smell in this room.

  他們試過把這間房間裡的味道清除掉。

- ∮ get along with 相處融洽

  We get along with our boss.

  我們跟老闆相處得很好。

- ∮ look down on 輕視

  You shouldn't look down on your brother.

  你不應該輕視你的弟弟。

- ∮ put up with 忍耐

  She can't put up with her noisy neighbors anymore.

  她再也受不了吵鬧的鄰居了。

- ∮ run out of 用盡

  She ran out of money, so she came back home.

  她錢花完了，只好回家。

- ∮ take care of 照顧，負責處理……

  I will take care of my dad's business.

  我將會管理父親的事業。

朗讀 CD 第 10 軌

互動光碟

4-1 生字 Vocabulary

argue	辯論（argue, argued, argued）
bad effect	壞的影響
ring	鈴響（ring, rang, rung）
pick up	拿起、接（人）（pick, picked, picked）
answer	回答（answer, answered, answered）
delightful	歡愉的，可愛的
tone	聲調
hang up	掛斷（電話）（hang, hung, hung）
order	命令（order, ordered, ordered）
tidy up	整理（tidy, tidied, tidied）
show up	出現（show, showed, showed/shown）
follow	隨著（follow, followed, followed）
among	在……之中
home-made	自家做的
taro cake	芋頭糕

steam	蒸（steam, steamed, steamed）
Taiwanese Sticky Rice	油飯
dig in	開始吃（dig, dug, dug）
remind	提醒（remind, reminded, reminded）
greeting	招呼，問候
chat	聊天（chat, chatted, chatted）
check out	看（check, checked, checked）
latest	最新的
adult	大人
exchange	交換（exchange, exchanged, exchanged）
home remedy	家傳祕方
share	分享（share, shared, shared）
lose weight	減肥（lose, lost, lost）

朗讀 CD 第 11 軌

互動光碟

4-2 課文 Text

While Mom and Dad were **arguing** about the **bad effects** of smoking, the telephone **rang**. Mom **picked up** the phone[1] and **answered** it, speaking in a **delightful**[2] **tone**. After **hanging up** the phone, she **ordered** Dad and me to **tidy up** the house because our uncle's family would visit[3] us this weekend.

On Saturday, my two cousins **showed up**[4] at the door first. My grandma, uncle, and aunt **followed** with bags of food in their hands. **Among**[5] those bags, I found my favorite[6] **home-made taro cakes** and **steamed**[7] **Taiwanese Sticky Rice**. As I was about to **dig in**[8], Mom **reminded** me to wait.

After a warm **greeting**[9] and **chatting** awhile, my cousins went into my room to **check out** my latest computer game. The **adults**, on the other hand[10], **exchanged** ideas on some **home remedies**[11]. While my aunt was happily **sharing** her new way of **losing weight**[12], Dad was listening quietly to his mother-in-law[13] talk about how to quit smoking.

4-3 課文翻譯

　　爸媽正在爭論抽菸的壞處時，電話鈴響了。媽媽接起電話，用很愉悅的聲音講著電話。她掛上電話後，指揮我和爸爸打掃房間，因為舅舅一家人這個週末要來看我們。

　　星期六兩個表弟妹先出現在我們家門口。阿嬤、舅舅和舅媽手中提著大包小包的食物也隨後趕到。在這些袋子裡面，我找到我最愛吃的手工芋頭糕和油飯，我正要開始吃的時候，媽媽提醒我等一等。

　　等大家打完招呼、寒暄一陣後，我的堂弟妹到我房間來看我新買的電腦遊戲。而另一方面，大人們則在交換著自家祕方。舅媽開心地分享她新的減肥方法，爸爸則安靜地聽他岳母告訴他如何戒菸。

朗讀 CD 第 12 軌

4-4 解析 Language Focus

互動光碟

1. phone 的相關片語

   ♪ pick up the phone 拿電話

   ♪ answer the phone 接電話

   ♪ talk on the phone 講電話

   ♪ hang up the phone 掛電話

2. delight 名詞，delightful 形容詞

   ♪ Everyone screamed with <u>delight</u> after hearing the good news.
   聽到這個大好消息，每個人高興得大叫。

   ♪ She is the most <u>delightful</u> person I have ever met.
   她是我見過最可愛的人。

3. visit 可以是拜訪一個人：

   ♪ He will visit his brother today.

   visit 也可以是到一個地方去旅行：

   ♪ I will visit Japan next week.

   visit 也可以是上一個網站：

   ♪ I often visit this website.

4. show up（出現）和 show off（愛現）都是動詞片語，但意思不同。

   ♪ He showed up at the last minute.
   最後一分鐘時他出現了。

♪ She likes to show off her new bike.
她喜歡炫耀她的新腳踏車。

5. among 三個以上中的一個：

♪ It's hard to choose from among these three.
要在這三個之中選一個很難。

between 兩個中的一個

♪ It's hard to choose from between these two.
要在這兩個之中選一個很難。

6. favorite 最喜歡：

♪ She is my favorite actress.
她是我最喜歡的女明星。

least favorite 最不喜歡：

♪ This is my least favorite movie.
這是我最不喜歡的電影。

7. steamed 是動詞 steam 的第三態變化，為過去分詞當形容詞用，帶有被動意味。steamed sticky rice 蒸熟的糯米飯。

8. dig in 開始吃。開飯前可以說： ♪ Dig in! 開動！

9. greet 打招呼（動詞），greeting 打招呼（名詞）

♪ We greet each other every morning.
我們每天早上互相打招呼。

♪ He raised a hand in greeting.
他舉起一隻手打招呼。

10. on the one hand 一方面來說，on the other hand 但是另外一方面來說（話又說回來）

♪ On the one hand, driving a car to work can save lots of time; on the other hand, it wastes lots of energy.（on the one hand 可以省略不用。）
一方面來說，開車上班很省時，但話又說回來，開車會浪費能源。

11. home remedy 自家的民間療法，家傳祕方。

　　🦻 Try this home remedy for your cold.
　　　試試這個家傳祕方來治你的感冒。

12. to lose weight 減肥（動詞），weight loss 減肥（名詞）

　　🦻 This <u>weight loss</u> center helps many people to <u>lose weight</u>.
　　　這家減肥中心幫很多人減重。

13. Family Relationship Words 親屬關係稱謂表

🦻
grandma, grandpa 祖父母，外祖父母（→grandparents 複數）
granddaughter, grandson 孫女、外孫女，孫子、外孫（→grandchildren 複數）
uncle 叔叔、伯伯、舅舅、姨丈、姑丈
aunt 嬸嬸、伯母、舅媽、阿姨、姑姑
cousin 堂兄弟姊妹、表兄弟姊妹
mother-in-law, father-in-law 岳母、婆婆，岳父、公公（＝in-laws 岳父母、公婆）
son-in-law 女婿
daughter-in-law 媳婦
sister-in-law 嫂嫂、大姑、小姑、弟妹
brother-in-law 大伯、姊夫、妹夫、小叔
nephew 姪子、外甥
niece 姪女、外甥女
stepmother, stepfather 繼母，繼父
stepsister, stepbrother 繼父與其前妻（或繼母與其前夫）所生之子女間的關係
half-brother, half-sister 同父異母或同母異父的兄弟姊妹

4-5-1 填填看

1. My mother's mother is my _____.

2. My aunt's daughter is my _____.

3. His daughter's husband is his _____.

4. Her aunt's daughter is her _____.

5. My sister's husband is my _____.

6. My brother's daughter is my _____.

7. Your father's brother is your _____.

8. Your uncle's son is your _____.

9. His wife's parents are his _____.

10. Her husband's sister is her _____.

11. She is her grandpa's _____.

12. Their son's wife is their _____.

13. Our sister's son is our _____.

14. Our uncle's children are our _____.

15. My mom's brother is my _____.

16. My father's mom is my mom's _____.

17. My sister's daughter is my _____.

18. My father's parents are my _____.

19. Your aunt's daughter is your _____.

20. You and your brothers and sisters are your grandparents' _____.

4-5-2 選擇適當的片語填入空格中

tidy up,   showed up,   check out,   lose weight,   home remedy,
get along,   dig in,   put up with,   listen to,   running out of

1.   She likes to _____ classical music（古典音樂）in her spare time.

2.   She and her stepdaughter _____alright. They rarely fight.

3.   Try this _____ to see if it will soothe（減輕）your pain.

4.   You need to _____ your room today. It's very messy.

5.   I had waited for a long time, but he never _____.

6.   Let's _____ this movie tonight.

7.   The food is ready. Let's _____.

8.   I can't _____ this lousy food（很糟的食物）anymore.

9.   Hurry up! we are _____ time!

10. They tried to _____ by walking 5 miles a day.

4-5-3 問答

1.   When the telephone rang, what did Mom do?

    _____

2.   What did she do after she hung up the phone?

    _____

3.   When would the uncle's family visit them?

    _____

4.   Who showed up at the door first on Saturday?

    _____

5. What were uncle, zuntie and grandma carrying in their hands?

   _____

6. What are the writer's favorite homemade foods?

   _____

7. When the writer was about to dig in, what happened?

   _____

8. What did his cousins do in his room?

   _____

9. What did the adults do while the children were playing computer games?

   _____

10. What did grandma tell the writer's dad?

   _____

4-5-4 改錯

1. Her mother looks her children after.
2. I can't put her up with anymore.
3. You shouldn't look down your little sister.
4. I will take care your dog when you are away.
5. When he ran out money, he came home.
6. I like this delight music.
7. He has lose a lot of weight.
8. Every time I say something, she is copy me.
9. You must to pick her up at 4 o'clock at the High Speed Rail Station（高鐵車站）.
10. They are always exchange the latest news.

4-5-5 英文該怎麼寫?

1. 她每次打電話來,我都不想接(...I don't feel like...)。

_____

2. 他剛掛了電話就打開電視看脫口秀(talk show)。(Right after...)

_____

3. 媽媽提醒我週末去拜訪我的老師。(Mom reminded...)

_____

4. 紅、藍、白三種顏色中,我最喜歡的是白色。(Among the colors...)

_____

5. 我的表弟正坐在舒服的長沙發上吃芋頭糕。

_____

6. 他試了各式各樣的家傳祕方來減肥。(He has tried all kinds of...)

_____

7. 我不知道他什麼時候才會出現(show up)。

_____

8. 他們正在討論看電視對小孩的不良影響(bad effects of...)。

_____

9. 我的阿姨們正在交換家傳祕方。

_____

10. 他岳母叫(ordered)他去清理他的房間。

_____

答案請見 pp. 163-164

動詞──容易混淆的動詞

互動光碟

　　不同動詞容易遭混淆的原因不一，有的是因為外型很像，如 fall, fell, fallen（跌倒）和 feel, felt, felt（覺得）這兩組意思完全不一樣的動詞，只因為拼法相似，而常遭誤用。有的動詞中文意思相似，如 borrow（向別人借）和 lend（借給別人），因為中文意思都是「借」，也常遭誤用。有的則是與其他詞類拼法相似，如「建議」這個字的動詞 advise 和名詞 advice 也常讓人分辨不清。現在將這三類容易混淆的動詞，選擇常遭誤用的例子，分別說明如下：

I. 拼法相似的動詞

1. a. fall, fell, fallen, falling（跌倒）

   My grandma fell and sprained her ankle.
   我的阿嬤跌倒而扭傷了腳踝。

   b. feel, felt, felt, feeling（覺得）

   I felt disappointed because I didn't get the job.
   因為沒有得到那份工作，我覺得很失望。

2. a. lie, lied, lied, lying（說謊）

   I didn't lie to her.
   我沒有對她說謊。

   I am not lying.
   我不是在說謊。

   b. lie, lay, lain, lying（躺）

   He often lies down and falls asleep right away.
   他常常一躺下來馬上就睡著了。

   He is lying on the couch.
   他正躺在長沙發上。

    c. lay, laid, laid, laying（放置）

She <u>laid</u> flowers on the table.

她把花放在桌上。

She is <u>laying</u> some paper on the floor.

她正在把一些紙鋪在地板上。

3. a. rise, rose, risen（升起、起身、起床）

He <u>rose</u> slowly from the chair.

他慢慢從椅子上站起來。

    b. raise, raised, raised（舉起、養育）

When the teacher asks a question, many students <u>raise</u> their hands.

老師問問題時，許多學生都舉手。

4. a. hang, hanged, hanged（絞死、吊死）

Saddam Hussein has been <u>hanged</u>.

海珊已被處絞刑。

    b. hang, hung, hung（掛）

He <u>hung</u> his clothes on the balcony.

他把衣服掛在陽台上。

He likes to <u>hang around</u> with his friends at the café after work.

下班後他喜歡跟朋友在咖啡店裡混。

5. a. adapt, adapted, adapted（使適用於……、改編）

We have to <u>adapt</u> ourselves <u>to</u> the new situation.

我們必須適應新的情況。

The movie <u>is adapted from</u> a novel.

這部電影是由小說改編而成。

b. adopt, adopted, adopted（採用、領養）

They <u>adopted</u> a new budget for the next three years.

他們採用了一個為未來三年所規劃的新預算。

II. 易與其他詞類相混淆的動詞

1. a. affect, affected, affected（影響，動詞）

His parents' divorce has <u>affected</u> him deeply.

他父母的離婚對他影響很深。

b. effect（影響，名詞）

The divorce has caused long-lasting <u>effects</u> on him.

離婚對他造成長遠的影響。

2. a. breathe, breathed, breathed（呼吸，動詞）

He <u>breathed</u> deeply and evenly.

他呼吸既深且勻。

b. breath（呼吸，名詞）

He took a deep <u>breath</u>, then began to climb the stairs.

他深呼吸了一下，然後開始爬樓梯。

3.　a.　choose, chose, chosen(選擇，動詞)

　　　I decided to <u>choose</u> this school for college.

　　　我決定選這所學校唸大學。

　　b.　choice(選擇，名詞)

　　　This is my final <u>choice</u>.

　　　這是我最後的選擇。

4.　a.　complain, complained, complained(抱怨，動詞)

　　　Don't <u>complain</u>. Just do it.

　　　不要抱怨。做就對了。

　　b.　complaint(抱怨，名詞)

　　　There are lots of <u>complaints</u> from the audience.

　　　觀眾有很多抱怨。

5.　a.　advise, advised, advised(建議，動詞)

　　　They <u>advised</u> us to leave here as soon as possible.

　　　他們建議我們儘快離開這裡。

　　b.　advice(建議，名詞，不可數)

　　　Take my <u>advice</u> and leave him immediately.

　　　接受我的建議馬上離開他。

III. 因中文意思相似而造成混淆的動詞：

1.　a.　borrow, borrowed, borrowed(向人借)

　　　I never <u>borrow</u> money <u>from</u> other people.

　　　我從不向人借錢。

b. lend, lent, lent(借給人)

I lent my old textbook to him.

我把我的舊課本借給他了。

2. a. take, took, taken(帶走)

b. bring, brought, brought(帶回)

The bus takes them to the park and brings them back.

巴士載他們去公園並且載他們回來。

3. a. see, saw, seen(不需費力,自然地「看」到)

I saw a man walking towards me.

我看到一個人正向我走來。

b. watch, watched, watched(觀察,注意)

I watched him talk with a girl.

我觀察他跟一個女孩說話。

c. look, looked, looked(往某個方向看)

If you look in that direction, you will see him standing there.

如果你往那個方向看,你會看到他站在那兒。

4. a. hear, heard, heard(不需費力,自然地聽到)

Did you hear what I said?

你聽到我說的了嗎?

b. listen, listened, listened(聆聽)

No, I didn't <u>hear</u>. I was <u>listening</u> to the music.

沒有耶，我沒聽到。我正在聽音樂。

5. a. realize, realized, realized(發現、了解到、意識到、領悟到)

As soon as they <u>realized</u> their mistake, they apologized right away.

他們一察覺到是他們的錯，就立刻道歉。

b. know, knew, known(認識、知道)

They don't <u>know</u> my name.

他們不知道我的名字。

6. a. live, lived, lived(住)

I have <u>lived</u> here for 30 years.

我已經住在這裡30年了。

b. stay, stayed, stayed(短期停留)

We visited Taichung and <u>stayed</u> there for two nights.

我們去台中玩，住了兩個晚上。

朗讀 CD 第 13 軌

互動光碟

5-1 生字 Vocabulary

relative	親戚
stay overnight	過夜（stay, stayed, stayed）
lie	躺（lie, lay, lain）
fall asleep	睡著了（fall, fell, fallen）
report	報告
quality	特質，特性
the Internet	網路
modern	現代的
world	世界
surprise	驚訝
break down	壞了（break, broke, broken）
call out	大叫（call, called, called）
rise	起床（rise, rose, risen）
get rid of	丟掉（get, got, got/gotten）
program	程式
complain	抱怨（complain, complained, complained）

advise	建議（advise, advised, advised）
in fact	事實上
online	線上，網路
affect	影響（affect, affected, affected）
studies	讀書、求學（用複數）

朗讀 CD 第 14 軌

互動光碟

5-2 課文 Text

Our **relatives stayed overnight**[1]. After they left, I heard Mom and Dad **lie** down on the bed[2] and chat about the fun parts of their visit[3]. A few minutes later, they **fell asleep**. I still couldn't go to bed because I had to finish a **report** about the good **qualities** of **the Internet**[4] in the **modern world**.

When I turned on the computer, to my **surprise**[5], nothing showed up. "Dad, my computer has **broken down**[6]!" I **called out**. Dad **rose** from the bed and turned my computer on again. He first **got rid of**[7] some of my computer game **programs**. Then, he **complained** that I spend[8] too much time playing games and **advised** me to quit playing[9] them.

Dad's complaint[10] was right. I did lie to him about using the computer to do homework. **In fact**, I was playing **online** games. If I continue doing this, it[11] will **affect** my life and my **studies**.

5-3 課文翻譯

　　我們的親戚在我家住了一晚。他們走後，我聽到爸媽躺在床上閒聊他們來訪的趣事。幾分鐘後，他們就睡著了。我還不能上床睡覺，因為我還得寫完一篇關於當代網路好處的報告。

　　當我打開電腦時，令我吃驚的是，沒有東西出現。我大叫：「爸，我的電腦壞啦！」爸從床上爬起來，把我的電腦重新開機。他先刪除一些我的電腦遊戲程式。接著他抱怨我花太多時間玩電玩，並建議我戒電玩。

　　爸爸的抱怨很對。我的確騙他我在用電腦做功課，其實，我是在玩線上遊戲。如果我繼續這麼做的話，它將會影響我的生活和學業。

朗讀 CD 第 15 軌

5-4 解析 Language Focus

互動光碟

1. 這裡的 relatives（親戚）是指作者的 grandma, uncle, aunt 和 cousins。他們只住了一晚，短暫的「住」用 stay 而不用 live。

2. hear 是感官動詞，後面接原形動詞 lie 和 chat。

* 注意：lie（躺）的動詞三態是：lie, lay, lain

3. the fun parts of their visit 是指「親戚來訪過程中的有趣部分」。

   ... of ... 是「所有格」的表達方式之一，如 Mary's chair = the chair of Mary

4. surf 有「瀏覽」的意思，常見用法有 surf the Internet（上網）和 on the Internet（網路上），記得 Internet 首字母要大寫才是標準寫法。

   🎧 He surfs the Internet every day.
   他每天上網（瀏覽網頁）。

   🎧 He found lots of information on the Internet.
   他在網路上找到許多資訊。

5. to my surprise 讓我吃驚的是……

   🎧 To my surprise, she didn't show up.
   讓我吃驚的是，她沒有出現。

   to my delight 讓我高興的是……

   🎧 To my delight, many of my students showed up.
   讓我高興的是，許多我的學生都來了。

   to my disappointment 讓我失望的是……

   🎧 To my disappointment, no one showed up.
   讓我失望的是，一個人都沒有出現。

6. break（破壞）的三態變化是 break, broke, broken，而動詞片語 break down 「是指電腦零組件壞掉而故障」，crash 則指電腦軟體出了問題而當機。

   🎵 My computer often breaks down.
      我的電腦常故障。（指零組件的問題。）

   🎵 My computer often crashes.
      我的電腦常當機。（指軟體的問題。）

7. get rid of 是三個字的動詞片語，這裡的意思與 delete 一樣。

   🎵 He got rid of my computer game programs.
      他把我的電腦遊戲程式殺掉了。

   🎵 He deleted the software.
      他刪除了這個軟體。

8. spend too much time playing game 是陳述一個「事實」，用現在式。

* 注意：spend 後面動詞要用動名詞。如：

   🎵 I spent the whole night doing my homework.
      我花了一整晚寫我的回家功課。

9. advise＋人＋to＋V. 建議某人（做）……

   🎵 He advised me to get to school on time.
      他建議我準時到校。

   quit + V-ing 戒掉……，停止（做）……

   🎵 He quit drinking Coke.
      他不再喝可口可樂了。

10. complaint（名詞）／complain（動詞）

   所有格後面要用名詞，如：

   🎵 His complaint made her angry.
      他的抱怨讓她生氣。

11. this 和 it 都指的是 playing online games。

5-5-1 選選看

1. I have _____ my key.

    (a) loss   (b) lost   (c) lose

2. He always _____ about our work.

    (a) complain   (b) complaint   (c) complains

3. Have you _____ asleep during a good movie?

    (a) fall   (b) felt   (c) fallen

4. They gave me a lot of _____.

    (a) advices   (b) advice   (c) advise

5. I _____ him NT$1000 last week, but he must have forgotten about it.

    (a) lent   (b) borrowed   (c) lend

6. Her computer _____ down a lot.

    (a) broken   (b) breaks   (c) breaking

7. She spends too much time _____ on the bed.

    (a) lying   (b) laying   (c) to lie

8. Mary went to bed and _____ asleep right away.

    (a) falling   (b) felt   (c) fell

9. She _____ that he didn't love her anymore.

    (a) fell   (b) feel   (c) felt

10. I don't mean to _____ to her.

    (a) laid   (b) lied   (c) lie

11. Watch out! Don't _____ your book on that machine(機器).

　　(a)lie　(b)lay　(c)laid

12. Don't _____ your wet clothes in the bathroom.

　　(a)hung　(b)hang　(c)hanging

13. I visited Singapore and _____ there for three days.

　　(a)live　(b)stay　(c)stayed

14. To my _____, he didn't answer my phone call.

　　(a)disappointment　(b)disappointing　(c)disappointed

15. Eating too much fast food will _____ your health.

　　(a)effect　(b)affect　(c)affects

5-5-2 填填看（選適當的字填入空格中）

raised, rise, lie, lay, affect, effects, hang, hung, advised, advice

1. He didn't follow the _____ his father gave him.

2. She _____ her hand, but the teacher didn't see it.

3. They always _____ up early but go to bed late.

4. They all _____ me not to drop out of school.

5. Did his comments _____ your decision?

6. Last night he _____ around with his friends at the KTV.

7. What are the good _____ of home schooling(在家教育)?

8. She likes to _____ newspapers on the floor.

9. I always _____ in bed for a long time but can't fall asleep.

10. Don't _____ your bag on the wall.

5-5-3 問答

1. How many nights did the relatives stay?

    _____

2. What did Mom and Dad do after our relatives left?

    _____

3. Why couldn't the writer go to bed when his parents fell asleep?

    _____

4. What surprised the writer?

    When he turned on _____

5. Who helped him fix(修理)the computer?

    _____

6. How did he fix the computer?

    _____

7. What did his dad complain about?

    _____

8. What did his dad advise him to do?

    _____

9. What did the writer lie to his dad about?

    _____

10. What will happen if the writer continues playing computer games?

    _____

5-5-4 改錯

1. She is laying on the bed reading a novel.

2. I fell that she didn't lie to me.

3. Which book did you choice?

4. He hanged his shirt on the balcony a week ago.

5. We have to adopt ourselves to the modern world.

6. Losing weight has had some bad affects on her health.

7. She gave me a lot of good advices.

8. Our boss never listens to our complains.

9. We visited Hualian and lived in a cheap hotel for three days.

10. They borrowed a book to me and asked me to return it in three days.

5-5-5 英文該怎麼寫？

1. 他們正躺在床上聽音樂。

   _____

2. 我住在朋友家兩晚。

   _____

3. 他給我許多有用的(useful)建議。

   _____

4. 我舉起手來回答問題(answer the question)。

   _____

5. 我跟他借了台幣100元。

   _____

6. 他選了這本英文小說來讀。

   _____

7. 玩電腦遊戲影響我的工作。

   _____

8. 我打開電腦，沒有東西出現。

_____

9. 最後我們的親戚都睡著了。

_____

10. 我的嬸嬸建議我戒玩電腦遊戲。

_____

答案請見 pp. 165-166

第六課 Unit 6

形容詞

互動光碟

形容詞通常指描述某個人、事或東西的字。例如:

✙ an old man(一位老人),是指 The man is old.

✙ a smart woman(一個聰明的女性),是指 The woman is smart.

✙ a used car(一部中古車),是指 The car is used.

✙ a brave girl(一位勇敢的女孩),是指 The girl is brave.

✙ a tall basketball player(一位高的籃球員),是指 The basketball player is tall.

上面畫橫線的字,如 old, smart, used, brave, tall 都是形容詞,而且每一個名詞的形容詞只一個,但有時可以用兩、三個形容詞來形容一個名詞,例如:

✙ a beautiful, old chair
一張美麗的舊椅子

✙ a big, square, purple plate
一個方形紫色的大盤子

或用一連串的形容詞來形容一個名詞,但這種機會並不多見。例如:

✙ an expensive, small, round, white pearl
一顆昂貴、小而圓的白珍珠

✙ an enormous, fresh, colorful Thai dish
一道份量超多、新鮮、色彩繽紛的泰國菜

當許多形容詞修飾一個名詞時,形容詞的排列有一定的次序,如"a green German sports car",我們不會說成"a sports German green car","her big wooden house",不會說成"her wooden big house",下

面的圖表整理出一個形容詞的排列順序，不過我們通常很少用一長串的形容詞來形容一個名詞。

形容詞排列順序							
限定詞	評斷	外觀敘述				地方	材質
		大小	形狀	年紀	顏色		
this	beautiful	small	round	old	red	Italian	wooden

形容詞通常放在被形容的名詞前面，但有些字如 something, someone, anybody，形容詞通常會擺在這些字的後面，例如：

🎵 Something good will appear.
好的東西會出現。

🎵 Someone nice will understand.
好的人會了解。

🎵 Anybody capable will get the job.
任何能幹的人都會得到這份工作。

有些形容詞可以從它的尾巴(-able, -al, -ful, -ic, -ive, -less, -ous)看出它是形容詞，請看下列圖表：

-able/-ible	remarkable, responsible, impossible, reliable...
-al	functional, external, logical, normal...
-ful	beautiful, careful, harmful, grateful...
-ic	terrific, fantastic, manic...
-ive	tentative, inventive, creative, persuasive...
-less	careless, restless, breathless...
-ous	humorous, courageous, fabulous...

記形容詞最好的方法是正、反詞一起記，如：

hot（熱的）	⟷	cold（冷的）
beautiful（美的）	⟷	ugly（醜的）
slow（慢的）	⟷	quick（快的）
clean（乾淨的）	⟷	dirty（骯髒的）
quiet（安靜的）	⟷	noisy（吵鬧的）
crowded（擁擠的）	⟷	empty（空的）
expensive（貴的）	⟷	cheap（便宜的）
complicated（複雜的）	⟷	simple（簡單的）
tall（高的）	⟷	short（矮的）
thick（厚的）	⟷	thin（薄的）
hard（硬的）	⟷	soft（軟的）
safe（安全的）	⟷	dangerous（危險的）
difficult（困難的）	⟷	easy（容易的）
long（長的）	⟷	short（短的）
wide（寬的）	⟷	narrow（窄的）

有些形容詞的相反詞可以從字首分辨出來，例如：

I.   加 "un" 字首的相反詞：

lucky（幸運的）	⟷	unlucky（不幸運的）
aware（意識到的）	⟷	unaware（沒意識到的）
comfortable（舒服的）	⟷	uncomfortable（不舒服的）
happy（快樂的）	⟷	unhappy（不快樂的）
safe（安全的）	⟷	unsafe（不安全的）

II. 加"dis"字首的相反詞：

honest（誠實的）　　⟷　　dishonest（不誠實的）

loyal（忠實的）　　⟷　　disloyal（不忠實的）

satisfied（滿意的）　⟷　　dissatisfied（不滿的）

* 注意 dissatisfied 表「不滿的」，與 unsatisfied（未得到滿足的）意思有些不同，例如：

I am dissatisfied with what he did.

我對他所做的事不滿意。

My passion for work is unsatisfied.

我對工作的熱情沒有得到滿足。

III. 加"im"字首的相反詞：

polite（禮貌的）　　⟷　　impolite（不禮貌的）

possible（可能的）　⟷　　impossible（不可能的）

IV. 加"in"字首的相反詞：

active（活躍的）　　⟷　　inactive（不活躍的）

considerate（體貼的）⟷　　inconsiderate（不顧別人的）

convenient（方便的）⟷　　inconvenient（不方便的）

V. 加"il"或 "ir"字首的相反詞：

legal（合法的）　　⟷　　illegal（不合法的）

regular（規則的）　⟷　　irregular（不規則的）

形容詞有時會以原級、比較級和最高級的面貌出現：例如：

He is young.

他很年輕。

🔊 He is <u>younger than</u> his classmates.
他比他的同學年紀都小。

🔊 He is my <u>younger</u> brother.
他是我的弟弟。

🔊 He is <u>the youngest</u> in our class.
他是我們班上年紀最小的。

* 注意：形容詞比較級後面通常加 "than"，形容詞最高級前面加 "the"。

一般一個音節（如 clean, old, safe）或兩個音節（narrow, shallow, gentle）的形容詞比較級只要在字尾加 -er，最高級加 -est：如

clean（乾淨的） →	cleaner than →	the cleanest
old（老、舊的） →	older than →	the oldest
safe（安全的） →	safer than →	the safest
narrow（窄的） →	narrower than →	the narrowest
shallow（淺的） →	shallower than →	the shallowest
gentle（溫柔的） →	gentler than →	the gentlest

* 注意：當兩個東西相互比較時，我們會用「形容詞比較級＋than」，如：

🔊 His room is <u>cleaner than</u> his brother's.
他的房間比他哥哥的乾淨。

但很多比較級的句型並沒有比較兩樣東西，因此不必加 than，例如：

🔊 I want a <u>cleaner</u> glass.
我要一個比較乾淨的玻璃杯。

有些一個或兩個音節的形容詞，字尾是 "y"，變成比較級時，必須去 "y" 再加 "-ier"；變成最高級時，必須去 "y" 再加 "-iest"。例如：

dry（乾的）	→	drier than	→	the driest
shy（害羞的）	→	shier than	→	the shiest
sly（狡猾的）	→	slier than	→	the sliest
funny（好笑的）	→	funnier	→	the funniest
happy（快樂的）	→	happier than	→	the happiest
dirty（髒的）	→	dirtier than	→	the dirtiest
healthy（健康的）	→	healthier than	→	the healthiest
hungry（餓的）	→	hungrier than	→	the hungriest

有些單音節的形容詞（如 sad、dim、flat），母音為短母音，加 "-er" 和 "-est" 時要重複後面的子音。例如：

sad（悲傷的）	→	sadder than	→	the saddest
dim（暗的）	→	dimmer than	→	the dimmest
flat（平坦的）	→	flatter than	→	the flattest

有些形容詞有兩個以上的音節（如 beau ti ful、ex pen sive、im por tant），變成比較級時不能加 "-er"，而是在形容詞前面加 more，變成最高級時不能在字後面加 "-est"，而要在前面加 the most，如：

beautiful（美麗的）	→ more beautiful than	→ the most beautiful
expensive（昂貴的）	→ more expensive than	→ the most expensive
important（重要的）	→ more important than	→ the most important

有些形容詞的比較級和最高級的變化不依照以上任何規則，請讀者背下來：

good（好的）	→ better than	→ the best
bad（壞的）	→ worse than	→ the worst
little（少的）	→ less than	→ the least
few（少的）	→ fewer than	→ the fewest
much（many, some）（多的）	→ more than	→ the most
far（遠的）	→ further than	→ the furthest

* 注意：far 的形容詞比較級可併作 farther；而形容詞最高級也可併作 the farthest

* 注意：不能在形容詞比較級前加 more，如：

📖 John's writing is ~~more~~ better than Peter's.
John 的作文比 Peter 的作文好。

📖 This summer is ~~more~~ hotter.
今年夏天比較熱。

朗讀 CD 第 16 軌

互動光碟

6-1 生字 Vocabulary

next door neighbor	隔壁鄰居
show	顯示（show, showed, showed/shown）
fluffy	毛絨絨的
stray cat	流浪貓
alley	巷弄
nearby	附近的
kitten	小貓
adorable	可愛的、迷人的
afford	買得起，抽得出（時間）（afford, afforded, afforded） * afford 這個動詞比較特別，通常與 can 連用，如：can afford 買得起、can't afford 買不起。過去式是 could afford、couldn't afford
extra	額外的
fall in love	愛上（fall, fell, fallen）
at first sight	第一眼
fur	毛

ink	墨（水）
crowded	擁擠的
towel	毛巾
private	私人的，個人專用的
bathroom	廁所，浴室
messy	髒亂的
playground	遊樂場
dine	進餐（dine, dined, dined）
touch	觸摸到（touch, touched, touched）
sticky	黏黏的
stand	容忍（stand, stood, stood）

朗讀 CD 第 17 軌

互動光碟

6-2 課文 Text

Today our **next door**[1] neighbor Mrs. Lin **showed** us a **fluffy** black **stray cat** she had picked up[2] in a quiet **alley nearby**. The Lins[3] are already raising three cute little **kittens**. Though[4] the others are not as **adorable** as[5] this one, the Lins really can't **afford**[6] an **extra** cat. My mom **fell in love** with[7] the kitten **at first sight**[8]. She decided to keep it and name it "Inky" since its **fur** is as dark as **ink**.

After adding[9] one more "member" to our family, the apartment has become very **crowded**. My mom used boxes and old **towels** to make a comfortable bed for Inky. She also set up[10] a **private**[11] **bathroom** for Inky.

Soon the nice clean space under the dining table became Inky's **messy**[12] **playground**. Whenever we **dine** together, our feet **touch sticky** things[13]. Dad couldn't **stand** it anymore. He said to Mom, "Look, this has become the dirtiest[14] spot in the house!"

6-3 課文翻譯

今天我們隔壁鄰居林太太給我們看一隻毛絨絨的黑色流浪貓，是她在附近一條安靜巷子裡撿到的。林家已經養了三隻可愛的小貓，雖然牠們不像這隻這麼可愛，但林家人真的沒辦法再多養一隻貓。媽媽第一眼就愛上了這隻貓。她決定叫牠「小墨」，因為牠的毛跟墨汁一樣黑。

我們家多了這位成員後，公寓變得很擁擠。媽媽用盒子和舊毛巾做了張舒服的小床給小墨。她還幫小墨搭建了一間專用廁所。

餐桌下面原本乾淨的地方很快就變成小墨髒亂的遊樂場。每次我們一起用餐時，我們的腳都會碰到黏黏的東西。爸爸再也受不了了，他跟媽媽說：「妳看，這裡已經變成屋子裡最髒的地方了！」

朗讀 CD 第 18 軌

互動光碟

6-4 解析 Language Focus

1. next door 在文中是形容詞，也可以寫成 next-door，而 next door 也當副詞用，如下列第二個例句。

   🔊 The house <u>next door</u> is empty.
   隔壁的房子是空的。

   🔊 We live <u>next door to</u> a convenience store.
   我們住在一家便利商店的隔壁。（next door to... 是片語。）

2. pick up 這個動詞片語我們在第四課已介紹過，pick up 有很多意思，例如：

   接人：

   🔊 I have to <u>pick up</u> my friend at the airport at 8:00. 我八點要去機場接朋友。

   撿起來：

   🔊 If you see litter on the floor, please <u>pick</u> it <u>up</u>.
   如果你在地上看到垃圾，請撿起來。

   習得：

   🔊 When did you <u>pick up</u> Spanish?
   你何時學會西班牙話的？

   課文中 showed us a cat 是過去發生的事，picked up a stray cat 也是過去發生的事，但是 picked up a cat 發生在 showed us a cat 之前，所以 picked up 要改為過去完成式 had picked up。

3. The Lins 指「林家人」，注意要加 s。如：The Smiths「史密斯這家人」，The Tanakas「田中這家人」。

4. though 指「雖然」，等同於 although，中文裡「雖然」後面常常接「但是」，所以學生寫英文句子時也常常將 thongh（although）和 but 併在一個句子裡出現，其實 though（although）後面不能接 but，如：

🎵 Though I love this dress, I don't think I can afford it.
　　雖然我愛這件洋裝，但是我覺得我買不起。

5. 如果兩個人、東西或事件很相似，我們可以用這個句型：as...as...「像……一樣」，例如：

🎵 His English is <u>as</u> <u>good</u> <u>as</u> mine（my English）.（as 和 as 中間用形容詞。）
　　他的英文跟我一樣好。

前面這個例句是肯定句，如果用在否定句，as...as... 有時可以改為 not as...as...。例如：

🎵 I am not <u>as</u> <u>tall</u> <u>as</u> she is.（as 和 as 中間用形容詞）
　　我不像她那麼高。

🎵 I don't walk <u>as</u> <u>fast</u> <u>as</u> she does.（as 和 as 中間用副詞）
　　我走得不像她那麼快。

as 和 as 中間也可以用形容詞＋名詞，例如：

🎵 I have <u>as</u> <u>many</u> <u>books</u> <u>as</u> she does.
　　我的書跟她一樣多。

🎵 I have <u>as</u> <u>much</u> <u>time</u> <u>as</u> she does.
　　我有跟她一樣多的時間。

＊ 注意：也許受中文的影響，許多學生常用一個錯誤的句型：as possible as...。

（×）　　　I study <u>as possible as</u> I can.

（○）🎵　I study <u>as</u> <u>hard</u> <u>as</u> I possibly can before every test.
　　　　每次考試前我盡可能努力用功讀書。

（○）🎵　I run <u>as</u> <u>hard</u> <u>as</u> I possibly can in each race I enter.
　　　　每次參加比賽時，我盡可能努力跑。

6. afford（動詞）付得起／affordable（形容詞）付得起的

🎧 We can't even afford to buy a sofa.
我們連一張沙發都買不起。

🎧 Chairs are affordable.
椅子還付得起(椅子價格很合理)。

7. 戀愛相關片語

🎧 fall in love with someone 愛上某人

🎧 have a crush on someone 迷戀某人

🎧 break up with someone 跟某人分手

8. sight 指視覺

🎧 His eyesight is poor. 他的視力不好。

🎧 He is nearsighted. 他近視。

🎧 He is farsighted. 他遠視。

🎧 love at first sight 一見鍾情

9. add...to...加某件東西在另外一件東西上，例如：

🎧 Add some salt and pepper to the soup.
在湯裡加點鹽和胡椒。

🎧 to add insult to injury
在傷口上撒鹽；落井下石；傷害之外又加污辱；雪上加霜

10. set up 是動詞片語，有幾個不同的用法：

🎧 The school set up a research center.
學校成立了一個研究中心。

🎧 He was set up by someone.
他遭人設計陷害。

🎧 software set-up
軟體裝置

11. private 私人的，個人專用的

> a private school 私立學校／a public school 公立學校
>
> a private hospital 私人醫院
>
> a private person 不多說自己事情的人
>
> a private place 一個安靜隱密的地方
>
> private lessons 為少數幾個學生設的小班，需付額外費用
>
> private things 私人物品
>
> invade my privacy 侵犯我的隱私權

12. messy（髒亂的，形容詞）／mess（混亂髒亂的東西，名詞）／mess up（弄亂，動詞片語）

> The house is a mess. = The house is messy.
> 房子亂成一團。

> He always messes up the room after I tidy it up.
> 我清好房間後，他老是會弄亂。

13. stick 黏（stick, stuck, stuck）是動詞，sticker「貼紙」，是名詞，sticky「很黏的」，是形容詞

以下是與 stick 相關的常用動詞片語：

> stick to learning English 一直學英文，永不放棄
>
> stick with your friend 跟朋友膩在一起或有福同享，有難同當
>
> collect stickers 收集貼紙
>
> sticky rice 糯米
>
> sticky rice balls 湯圓

14. dirty, dirtier than（骯髒的）, the dirtiest

> This T-shirt is dirty. 這件 T 恤很髒。

> This T-shirt is dirtier than that one. 這件 T 恤比那件髒。

> This is the dirtiest T-shirt. 這件 T 恤最髒。

6-5-1 選選看

1. This is the _____ (hard) book I have ever read.

   (a) hard　(b) harder (c) hardest

2. Why do you always make your room so_____

   (a) mess　(b) messy　(c) mess up

3. The teacher gave him a _____ when he answered the question correctly.

   (a) stick　(b) sticky　(c) sticker

4. The bus was very _____ today.

   (a) crowed　(b) crowded　(c) crowd

5. I feel _____ than beforc.

   (a) more hungrier　(b) hunger　(c) hungrier

6. She is _____ student in our class.

   (a) the healthiest　(b) the most healthy　(c) the healthy.

7. Your desk is tidier than _____.

   (a) her's　(b) her　(c) hers

8. Her health is _____ than before.

   (a) bad　(b) worser　(c) worse

9. This is _____ movie I have ever seen.

   (a) the worst　(b) worst　(c) the baddest

10. The street is much _____ now.

    (a) more quieter　(b) more quiet　(c) quieter

11. Have they ＿＿＿＿＿up a new center yet?

    (a) setted　(b) setting　(c) set

12. Let's stick ＿＿＿＿＿our old plan. Don't change it all the time.

    (a) to　(b) at　(c) up

13. She is not as ＿＿＿＿＿as she used to be.

    (a) younger　(b) young　(c) youngest

14. He tried to drive as ＿＿＿＿＿ as he could.

    (a) slow　(b) slower　(c) slowly

15. She drinks ＿＿＿＿＿water than she did before.

    (a) fewer　(b) little　(c) less

6-5-2 選出適當的形容詞填入句子中

messy, difficult, next door, expensive, adorable, private, sticky, fluffy, comfortable, crowded

1. This is our ＿＿＿＿＿＿ bathroom. It is not open to the public.

2. Our ＿＿＿＿＿＿ neighbor often borrows things from us but forgets to return them.

3. The house is too ＿＿＿＿＿＿. We really can't afford it.

4. I like to touch the ＿＿＿＿＿＿ white towel. It is so soft.

5. The ＿＿＿＿＿ baby is sleeping in her arms.

6. It is the most ＿＿＿＿＿＿ decision I have ever made.

7. She is lying on a ＿＿＿＿＿＿ couch.

8. He can't even find his pants. His room is so ＿＿＿＿＿＿.

9. The shopping mall(大型購物中心)is always ＿＿＿＿＿＿ on the weekend.

10. The candy is so ＿＿＿＿＿ that I can't get it of the box.

6-5-3 問答

1. Who is Mrs. Lin?

   She _____

2. What did she show to the writer's family?

   She showed them _____

3. Where did she find it?

   She found it _____

4. What color is the fur of the stray cat?

   Its fur _____

5. How many cats does Mrs. Lin have?

   She _____

6. What is the cat's name?

   Its _____

7. Why did they give it such a name?

   They named it _____ because _____

8. How did the writer's mom make a bed for the cat?

   She used _____

9. What happened to the space under the dining table?

   The space under the dining table _____

10. Why was the writer's dad angry?

    He was angry because _____

6-5-4 改錯

1. You always messy up the living room after I tidy it up.

2. I tried as possible as I could to learn English.

3. I am not as taller as she is.

4. She is smartest in our family.

5. Taipei 101 is higher building in Taiwan.

6. The teacher dissatisfied with students' performance（表現）.

7. My grandma is more healthier than before.

8. To open the door without knocking is very inpolite.

9. The apartment has become very crowd.

10. This towel is dryer than that one.

6-5-5 英文該怎麼寫？

1. 我在公園裡撿到一隻流浪貓。

   _____

2. 我好喜歡那隻白絨絨的狗。（be fond of）

   _____

3. 他給我看那間小而安靜的書房（study）。

   _____

4. 我隔壁的鄰居很吵。

   _____

5. 這張飯桌沒有那張那麼長。（not as...as）

   _____

6. 這是我們店裡最舒適的一張床。

   _____

7. 我和他花同樣多的時間讀英文。（I spend...）

   _____

8. 他無法忍受兒子髒亂的房間。（He can't stand...）

   _____

9. 我只買得起那台比較便宜的電腦。（I can only afford...）

　　_____

10. 雖然我一眼就愛上這隻流浪狗，但是我不能養牠(keep it)。

　　_____

答案請見 pp. 166-167

第七課 Unit 7

副詞

互動光碟

副詞用來形容「動詞」、「形容詞」、「副詞」或整個「句子」。例如：

🐚 He walks slowly.

他慢慢地走。（副詞 slowly 形容動詞 walk。）

🐚 She is terribly ill.

她病得很慘。（副詞 terribly 形容形容詞 ill。）

🐚 She sings very beautifully.

她唱得很美。（副詞 very 形容副詞 beautifully。）

🐚 Luckily, they did not go.

幸好他們沒去。（副詞 luckily 形容整個句子 They did not go.）

通常形容詞加上 "-ly" 就成了副詞，例如：

slow	→	slowly 慢慢地
serious	→	seriously 嚴肅地
confident	→	confidently 自信地
beautiful	→	beautifully 美麗地
skillful	→	skillfully 熟練地
original	→	originally 原來地
equal	→	equally 相等地
thoughtful	→	thoughtfully 體貼地
convenient	→	conveniently 方便的
independent	→	independently 獨立地

　　大部分的副詞都有一個尾巴 "-ly"，但也有一些例外，如 friendly（友善的）、lovely（可愛的）、lonely（寂寞的）、manly（有男子氣概的）看起來像是副詞，卻是形容詞。例如：

🎵 Mary is very <u>friendly</u>.
　　瑪麗很友善。（friendly 形容名詞 Mary。）

🎵 Mary treated me in a <u>friendly</u> way.
　　瑪麗待我很友善。（friendly 形容名詞 way；in a friendly way 形容動詞 treat。）

🎵 Amy is a <u>lovely</u> girl.
　　愛咪是個可愛的女孩。

　　也有許多副詞字尾沒有 "-ly"，有時候當形容詞用，有時候也當副詞用。例如：

🎵 He drives very <u>well</u>.
　　他車開得很好。（副詞 well 形容動詞 drive）

🎵 I am not very <u>well</u> today.
　　我今天身體不舒服。（形容詞 well 形容代名詞 I）

🎵 He studies <u>hard</u>.
　　他（很）用功讀書。（副詞 hard 形容動詞 study）

🎵 The work is <u>hard</u>.
　　這個工作很難。（形容詞 hard 形容名詞 work）

🎵 He arrived <u>late</u>.
　　他很晚才到。（副詞 late 形容動詞 arrive）

🎵 He was <u>late</u> for the test.
　　他考試遲到了。（形容詞 late 形容代名詞 he）

* 注意：hard 和 hardly 是兩個看起來相似，意思卻完全不同的字。
  形容詞 hard 的副詞也是 hard(難，努力)，不是 hardly。hardly 是
  「幾乎不」、「幾乎沒有」的意思。例如：

  🖐 I have <u>hardly</u> called him lately.
  　　最近我很少(幾乎不)打電話給他。

  🖐 I tried very <u>hard</u> to find him.
  　　我努力嘗試找到他。

* 注意：late 和 lately 也是兩個看起來相似，意思卻完全不同的字。
  形容詞 late 的副詞是 late(晚)，不是 lately。lately 是「最近」的
  意思。例如：

  🖐 He hasn't been good <u>lately</u>.
  　　他最近不太好。

  🖐 He has to work <u>late</u> at night.
  　　他晚上得工作到很晚。(late是形容動詞 work 的副詞。)

和形容詞一樣，副詞也有比較級，例如：

  🖐 She runs <u>faster</u> than her elder brother.
  　　她比她哥哥跑得快。(fast 是形容動詞 run 的副詞。)

  🖐 He started to drive <u>more slowly</u> after getting a ticket.
  　　吃了一張罰單後，他開始開得比較慢了。(slowly 形容
  　　drive，比較級是 more slowly。)

  🖐 Please speak <u>more slowly</u>.
  　　請說慢一點。

副詞也有最高級，例如：

🎧 He sings the most skillfully.
他唱得最有技巧。

🎧 The boss treats the staff the most terribly.
這位老闆對待員工最壞。

與 more 和 most 意思相反的比較級和最高級是 less 和 least，如：

🎧 He did it more carefully this time.
他這次做得比較小心。

🎧 He did it less carefully this time.
他這次做得比較不小心。

🎧 That was the work that he finished the most carefully.
那是他最小心完成的工作。

🎧 That was the work that he finished the least carefully.
那是他最不經心完成的工作。

as...as... 的中間可放入副詞，用來比較兩個等級相同的人、事、物，例如：

🎧 She can run as fast as her brother.
她跑得跟她哥哥一樣快。

🎧 She did as well as her brother.
她做得跟她哥哥一樣好。

朗讀 CD 第 19 軌

互動光碟

7-1 生字 Vocabulary

unusual	不尋常的
actually	竟然，居然
happily	快樂地
back and forth	來回地
rubber	橡膠
secretly	祕密地
take a look	看一看（take, took, taken）
really	很，十分
soft side	柔和的一面
disturb	打擾（disturb, disturbed, disturbed）
retreat	撤退（retreat, retreated, retreated）
suddenly	突然
by the time	當……的時候
voice message	語音留言
a bunch of	一群
sneakers	運動鞋
obviously	顯然地
get bored	覺得無聊（get, got, got/gotten）

朗讀 CD 第 20 軌

互動光碟

7-2 課文 Text

This morning something **unusual**[1] happened. I could hardly believe my eyes[2] — My dad was **actually**[3] playing with Inky! Listen to what he said: "Come here, Inky. Catch the ball." They were running **happily back and forth** around the living room, chasing a small **rubber** ball. I **secretly** called Mom to come and **take a look**. She was also **really** surprised[4] to see Dad's **soft side**.

We tried not to **disturb** him and Inky, but I couldn't help[5] laughing when Mom and I quietly **retreated** to the kitchen. **Suddenly**, I heard my cell phone ringing[6]. However, **by the time** I rushed to my room to answer it, the caller had hung up[7]. I checked the **voice message**; it was from Jie Ming, my junior high school classmate. He and **a bunch of**[8] friends were waiting for me at the school basketball courts[9]. I quickly put on my shorts and **sneakers**[10] and got ready to meet them.

I closed the door quietly, leaving[11] my parents behind to talk about their lovely Inky. **Obviously**, because of their common interest in Inky, they won't **get bored** for a while.

今早有件不尋常的事發生了，我幾乎不敢相信我看到的景象——爸爸居然跟小墨一起玩耍！你聽他怎麼說：「來這兒，小墨。接球！」他們在客廳裡高興地跑來跑去追一顆小橡皮球。我悄悄叫媽媽過來看。她也對爸爸柔性的一面感到很驚訝。

我們不想打擾他和小墨，但我和媽媽靜靜地退到廚房時，我忍不住笑了起來。突然，我聽到手機在響，當我跑到我的房間去接聽時，電話已掛斷了。我查了查手機留言，是我的國中同學傑明打來的。他正跟一群朋友在學校籃球場等我。我立刻穿上短褲和球鞋，準備去見他們。

我把門輕輕關上，留爸媽在屋裡談他們可愛的小墨。顯然地，因為他們對小墨同樣感興趣，他們好一陣子不會覺得無聊了。

朗讀 CD 第 21 軌

互動光碟

7-4 解析 Language Focus

1.　unusual 不平常的（形容詞）／unusually 不平常地（副詞）

　　◎　His parents are very unusual.
　　　　他的父母很不尋常。

　　◎　This event is unusually complicated.
　　　　這件事情異常複雜。（副詞 unusually 形容形容詞 complicated）

2.　can't believe one's eyes（不相信某人的眼睛），指「所見到的事情太奇怪了」。can't believe one's ears（不相信某人的耳朵），指「所聽到的事情太不可思議了」。

3.　actually（= in fact）在文中用以強調某件事情居然發生了。

　　◎　He actually hasn't slept for three days!
　　　　他居然三天沒睡！

　　副詞 actually 也可以放在句子前面，強調事情的真實性等同於 in fact。

　　◎　Actually, he spent a week finishing the work.
　　　　事實上，他花了一星期才完成這項工作。

　　也可以解釋自己真正的意思是什麼。

　　◎　Actually, I called you for some advice.
　　　　其實，我打電話給你是要問你一些意見。

4.　be really surprised 中的副詞 really 修飾形容詞 surprised

　　surprise 是動詞，surprised 為形容詞，指對什麼事情「感到驚訝的」，surprising 也是形容詞，但表示事情的本身是「令人驚訝的」。

♫ Seeing Dad's soft side really <u>surprises</u> Mom.
看到爸爸柔性的一面真令媽媽驚訝。

♫ Mom <u>is</u> really <u>surprised at</u> Dad's soft side.
媽媽對爸爸柔性的一面真的感到驚訝。

♫ Dad's soft side <u>is</u> really <u>surprising</u>.
爸爸柔性的一面真令人驚訝。

形容詞 surprising 的副詞是 surprisingly，例如：

♫ He performed <u>surprisingly</u> well this semester.
他這學期的表現出奇地好。

5. 動詞 help

♫ I helped him（to）set up his own blog.
我幫他架設好他自己的部落格。

♫ I took some medicine, but it didn't help.
我吃了些藥，卻沒用。

名詞 help

♫ I took some medicine, but it was not much help.
我吃了些藥，卻沒用。

♫ I desperately need your help.
我急需你的幫忙。

形容詞 helpful

♫ This medicine was very helpful.
這帖藥很有效。

6. hear 是感官動詞，三態變化為 hear, heard, heard，其後須接受詞，再接原形
動詞或 V-ing，如：

♫ I heard the telephone ring.
我聽到電話響了。

⟐ I heard the telephone ringing, but I couldn't pick it up.
我聽到電話正在響，但我沒辦法接。

7. hang up the phone 掛斷電話(動詞 hang 的三態變化為 hang, hung, hung)

⟐ She always hangs up the phone in a hurry before we finish our conversation.
她總是還沒講完就匆匆掛斷電話。

⟐ I hung up the phone when I finished the conversation.
我談完後掛斷電話。

⟐ The phone was hung up.
電話被掛斷了。

課文中這個句子有兩個發生在過去的動作：The caller hung up the phone.(打電話的人掛斷了電話)。I rushed to my room.(我急忙跑回房間)。兩個動作都發生在過去，但掛斷電話在先，所以掛斷電話這個動作要改為過去完成式：The caller had hung up...

8. a bunch of 可解釋為「一串」、「一群」、「一束」等，常見例子有：

⟐ a bunch of people
一群人

⟐ a bunch of flowers
一束花

⟐ a bunch of keys
一串鑰匙

⟐ a bunch of grapes
一串葡萄

⟐ a bunch of bananas
一串香蕉

9. court 指「球場」，如：basketball court(籃球場)、tennis court(網球場)，不過「保齡球場」是 bowling alley、「高爾夫球場」是 golf course。

10. sneakers 和 shorts 通常成對出現，所以要用複數。其他成對出現的詞如：glasses 眼鏡、goggles 蛙鏡、jeans 牛仔褲、socks 襪子、stockings 長襪、swimming trunks 游泳褲；如果要問上述某樣東西多少錢時，要說：How much are they?

11. leave（leave, left, left）有許多不同的意思，如：

離開：

🠒　I leave home at 7:30 every morning.
　　我每天早上 7：30 離開家。

把……交給：

🠒　I left my key with a neighbor.
　　我把我的鑰匙留給鄰居。

留下：

🠒　I left a message on her answering machine.
　　我在她的答錄機裡留言。

7-5-1 選選看

1. If something _____ happens, you can call me right away.
   (a) unusually　(b) unusual　(c) usual

2. _____, he is a nice boy.
   (a) Unusually,　(b) Really,　(c) Actually

3. I _____ called my boyfriend without being noticed.
   (a) secretly　(b) obviously　(c) beautifully

4. They can make computers more _____.
   (a) cheap　(b) cheaper　(c) cheaply

5. You must drive more _____.
   (a) careful　(b) care　(c) carefully

6. The book is the most _____ in the bookstore.
   (a) popularly　(b) popular　(c) popularity

7. She tried to work _____ in order to make more money.
   (a) more hardly　(b) more hard　(c) harder

8. My grandpa gets up the _____ in my family.
   (a) early　(b) earliest　(c) earlier

9. She can _____ finish the job without any problems.
   (a) ease　(b) easy　(c) easily

10. Something _____ happened, I have to call the police.
    (a) terrible　(b) terribly　(c) more terribly

11. The doctor said his condition is _____.

(a) seriously　(b) more seriously　(c) serious

12. Mom and Dad _____ told me stories about "Inky."

(a) happy　(b) happiness　(c) happily

13. She saw him _____ making dumplings in the kitchen.

(a) busily　(b) busy　(c) business

14. _____ , I am from Tainan, but now I am living in Taichung.

(a) Luckily,　(b) Originally,　(c) Happily

15. All of a sudden, they became _____ silent.

(a) usual　(b) unusually　(c) unusual.

7-5-2 問答

1. What kind of unusual thing happened?

   _____

2. How did the writer's father play with Inky?

   _____

3. What did the writer's father say to Inky?

   _____

4. What was the writer's mother so surprised at?

   _____

5. Where did the writer and his mom retreat to?

   _____

6. Who called the writer?

   _____

7. What was the text message about?

_____

8. What is the common interest of the writer's parents?

_____

7-5-3 改錯

1. Her graduation speech was surprising good.

2. Something terribly happened this morning.

3. I hang up the phone and ran over to meet her.

4. We quick retreated to a safer place.

5. He is easily get boring.

6. I can't help to feel sorry for the poor guy.

7. I felt terrible sorry about the incident.

8. He hid his diary at the secretly location.

9. I will meet a bunch of friend to play basketball.

10. If she drives more slowlier, I will be able to catch up with her.

7-5-4 英文該怎麼寫？

1. 我穿上短褲和球鞋去打籃球。

_____

2. 糟糕的事發生了，我得趕快離開。

_____

3. 他靜靜地退回自己的房間。

_____

4.　他開車跟他哥哥一樣慢。

_____

5.　我悄悄把這隻流浪貓藏在我的桌子下面。(hide, hid, hidden)

_____

6.　顯然地，他不想聽你要說的。

_____

7.　我查了一下簡訊，是我的表弟打來的。

_____

8.　事實上，我不喜歡這個最新的電腦遊戲。

_____

9.　他正舒服地坐在長沙發(couch)上讀一本小說。

_____

10.　他體貼地遞給我一杯豆漿。

_____

答案請見 pp. 167-168

第八課 Unit 8

助動詞

互動光碟

助動詞通常放在動詞前面，顧名思義，是用來幫助動詞，例如我們初級本學的 do 就是一個助動詞，它本身會隨著主詞而改變型態（如 I do..., She does...），但跟在它後面的動詞則永遠保持原形，不跟著主詞而變動。如：

🔊 Do you like to play the piano?
你喜歡彈鋼琴嗎？

🔊 Does she like to play the piano?
她喜歡彈鋼琴嗎？

＊ 助動詞 do 因主詞是第二人稱而用 do；主詞是第三人稱時而改用 does。動詞 like 則保持原形，不必因 she 是第三人稱而加 s，變成 likes。

中級本學的助動詞 have to 也會隨主詞人稱不同而變化，如：

🔊 I have to play basketball now.
我現在必須打籃球。

🔊 He has to play basketball now.
他現在必須打籃球。

＊ 助動詞 have to 因主詞是第一人稱而用 have to；若主詞是第三人稱就須改用 has to，但後面的動詞 play 則保持原形。

有些助動詞叫做語氣助動詞，如 will, may, might, can, could, must, should, would 都是語氣助動詞，跟 do 和 have to 這類助動詞不同，不會隨主詞人稱不同而改變型態，這些語氣助動詞後面的動詞也都用原形。如：

I		
You		
She		
He	<u>must</u>	go now.
It		
We		
You		
They		

　　語氣助動詞通常跟著動詞一起出現在句中，它們彼此的意思很接近，在某種情況下甚至可以互換著用，但要注意的是，即使意思完全一樣的兩個助動詞，如 can 和 could 用在懇請別人幫忙時，用 could 聽起來就比 can 來得婉轉、禮貌。以下是語氣助動詞的用法：

I. can

表示許可：

🎧　You <u>can</u> come with your sister.

　　= You <u>are allowed to</u> come with your sister.

　　你可以跟你的姊姊一起來。

表示能力：

🎧　She <u>can</u> play at least three instruments.

　　= She <u>is able to</u> play at least three instruments.

　　她至少會玩三種樂器。

表示請求：

🎧　<u>Can</u> you help me set up this software?

　　你可以幫我灌這個軟體嗎？

表示預測：

🔊 We <u>can</u> win the game if we try hard.
　　我們只要努力就一定會贏得這場比賽。

II. could

徵求許可：

🔊 <u>Could</u> I leave now?
　　我現在可以離開嗎？

表示可能性：

🔊 Who knows? He <u>could</u> be your future husband.
　　誰知道呢？他可能是妳未來的先生喔！

假設：

🔊 If I had more time, I <u>could</u> finish all the books on the bookshelf.
　　假如我有多餘的時間，我就能把書架上所有的書看完。

禮貌性地請求：

🔊 <u>Could</u> I borrow your stapler?
　　我可以跟你借釘書機嗎？

建議：

🔊 You <u>could</u> spend your vacation in Kenting.
　　你可以到墾丁去度假。

III. had better

勸告：

🔊 You <u>had better</u> learn some Japanese.
　　你最好學點日語。

強烈希望，甚至帶有警告的意味：

👂 They <u>had better</u> be here before we start dinner.
他們最好在我們開飯之前到！

IV. may

徵求許可：

👂 <u>May</u> I register tomorrow?
我可以明天註冊嗎？

給予許可：

👂 You <u>may</u> not leave the table before the other guests finish their meal.
你不能在其他客人用餐完畢前離開餐桌。

表示可能：

👂 It <u>may</u> be their last chance to win the game.
這可能是他們最後一次贏得這場比賽的機會。

猜測：

👂 She <u>may</u> be our next president.
她可能會是我們下一任總統。

V. might

也許：

👂 I <u>might</u> go to China this summer.
= I may go to China this summer.

今年夏天我也許會去中國。

假設：

🎵 If I stayed up late, I <u>might</u> finish the work.
如果我開夜車的話，也許做得完工作。

建議：

🎵 You <u>might</u> try the fruitcake.
= You <u>could</u> try the fruitcake.
你可以試試這個水果蛋糕。

建議（常以 may/might as well 表「最好還是……，還是……的好」，帶有「沒有理由不該這麼做，因為似乎沒有比這個更好的方法了」的含意）：

🎵 Gas prices are so high these days; you <u>might as well</u> get rid of your car and ride a bicycle instead.
最近油價這麼高，你最好還是把車賣掉，改騎腳踏車。

VI. must

必須：

🎵 You <u>must</u> take off your shoes before entering the house.
進屋前一定要脫鞋。

建議：

🎵 You <u>must</u> take some time off and get some rest.
= You <u>have to</u> take some time off and get some rest.
你一定要休假休息一下。

推斷：

🎵 You <u>must</u> be over 180 c.m. tall.
你身高一定超過180公分吧。

猜測：

🎧 I guess she <u>must</u> be your English teacher.

我猜她一定是你的英文老師。

VII. shall（通常只能與 I 和 we 在一起，較常出現在英式英文中）

邀約：

🎧 <u>Shall</u> we dance?

我可以邀你跳舞嗎？

建議：

🎧 <u>Shall</u> we move to the living room?

我們移到客廳好嗎。（把整個活動範圍移過去。）

VIII. should

推薦、建議：

🎧 If you go to Taichung, you <u>should</u> visit the Science Museum.

= If you go to Taichung, you <u>must</u> visit the Science Museum.

如果你去台中，應該去參觀科學博物館。

勸告：

🎧 You <u>should</u> quit playing computer games.

你應該不要再玩電腦遊戲了。

義務：

🎧 I <u>should</u> return the DVD before the DVD rental store closes.

我應該在 DVD 出租店關門前歸還這張 DVD。

表示期待或預測：

🎧 Her new novel <u>should</u> be released soon.
她的新小說應該快出版了吧！

表示猜測：

🎧 It's 8 o'clock. She <u>should</u> be here in a few minutes.
八點了。她應該幾分鐘之內就會到了。

IX. will

表現意志：

🎧 I <u>will</u> find a good job in the near future.
我最近就會找到一個好工作。

允諾：

🎧 I <u>will</u> call you tonight.
我今晚會打電話給你。

推測：

🎧 The clothes <u>will</u> not be ready by next week.
衣服下星期前還不會好。

禮貌懇求：

🎧 <u>Will</u> you stay for dinner?
你會留下來吃晚飯吧？

表未來：

🎧 The new bookstore <u>will</u> open on January 21st.
這家新書店會在1月21日開張。

X. would

推測:

🎧 It <u>would</u> cost much more for the five of us to take two taxis.
五個人搭兩輛計程車會貴很多。

假設:

🎧 If I were you, I <u>would</u> not go with him.
如果我是你的話,我不會跟他去的。

禮貌邀約:

🎧 <u>Would</u> you like to go with me?
你想跟我去嗎?

禮貌表達喜好:

🎧 I <u>would</u> love to have a cup of tea.
我想要喝杯茶。

禮貌懇請幫忙:

🎧 <u>Would</u> you help me lift this box up?
你可以幫我把這一箱抬上去嗎?

朗讀 CD 第 22 軌

互動光碟

8-1 生字 Vocabulary

scooter	機車
hallway	走廊
behind	後面
convenience store	便利商店
bottle	瓶
reluctantly	不情願地
firmly	堅定地
jam-packed	擠得滿滿的
player	打球的人、球員
middle-aged	中年的
text message	手機簡訊
in front of	在……前面（behind 在……後面）
gym	體育館、健身房
wave	揮（手）（wave, waved, waved）
indoor	室內（outdoor 室外）
familiar	熟悉的

take off	脫掉 (take, took, taken) (put on 穿上)
jacket	夾克、西裝上衣
join	加入 (join, joined, joined)

朗讀 CD 第 23 軌

互動光碟

8-2 課文 Text

As I was moving my **scooter** outside from the **hallway**, Mom called me from **behind**[1], "On your way back home, could you stop at a **convenience store** and buy a **bottle** of milk[2]?" she asked. "I might have to go somewhere after the basketball game, but I will try my best[3] to get one." I answered **reluctantly**[4]. "Well, young man, you must buy a bottle, or[5] we will have no milk tomorrow for our breakfast!" Mom said **firmly**[6].

The school basketball courts were **jam-packed**[7] with **players**. Some girls and **middle-aged**[8] men were among them. However, none[9] of them were my friends. There must be someone around here, I thought. Should[10] I call Jie Ming now? Will they send me a **text message**? I might as well just stand here to see what will happen.

Just then, I saw someone **in front of** the **gym**[11] **waving** to me. I knew it must be Jie Ming. I ran as fast as I could. In the **indoor** basketball court, I saw many **familiar** faces. I quickly **took off**[12] my **jacket** and **joined** the game.

　　當我正把機車從走廊移出去時，媽從後面把我叫住，問道：「回家的路上，你可以在便利商店停一下，買瓶牛奶嗎？」我心不甘情不願地回答說：「球賽結束後我可能得到別的地方去，但我會盡量買一瓶。」媽媽用堅定的語氣說：「喂，小子，你一定得買一瓶，否則明天早餐我們就沒有牛奶可喝了！」

　　學校籃球場擠滿了打球的人。其中也有些女孩和中年人。不過，沒有一個是我的朋友。我想一定有某個我的朋友在這附近。我現在該不該打電話給傑明呢？他們會不會傳簡訊給我？我最好還是站在這裡看看會發生什麼事。

　　就在這時候，我看到體育館前有人向我揮手。我知道一定是傑明！我儘快跑過去。在室內籃球場上，我看到許多熟悉的面孔。我迅速脫掉夾克，加入球賽。

朗讀 CD 第 24 軌

互動光碟

8-4 解析 Language Focus

1. 課文的第一句是典型的過去進行式，通常與過去式對照著用，例如：

   ☙ While I was taking a shower, the phone rang.
   我在沖澡時，電話鈴響了。

   ☙ As I was taking the test, my teacher called my name.
   我正在考試時，老師叫我的名字。

2. milk 是不可數名詞，不能加 s，想要計量 milk，可以用：

   ☙ a glass of milk
   一杯牛奶

   ☙ a bottle of milk
   一瓶牛奶

   ☙ a box of milk
   一盒牛奶

3. try one's best 和 do one's best 都可表示「盡某人最大的努力去做……」，也就是「盡力而為」、「盡己所能」。

4. reluctant（形容詞），reluctantly（副詞），reluctance（名詞）

   ☙ She was <u>reluctant</u> to lend him the money.
   她很不甘願借他錢。

   ☙ She answered the question <u>reluctantly</u>.
   她心不甘情不願地回答問題。

   ☙ She showed <u>reluctance</u> to lend him the money.
   她借錢給他時露出不甘願的樣子。

*　注意：reluctantly 的相反詞是 willingly（很願意地）

5.　or 是連接詞（第十課會詳細說明），有幾種不同的用法：

或是：

　♪　Would you like tea or coffee?
　　　你要茶還是咖啡？

不確定：

　♪　I have two or three options.
　　　我有兩、三個選擇。

否則：

　♪　You had better quit smoking, or you may get lung cancer.
　　　你最好戒煙，不然你可能會得肺癌。

6.　firm（形容詞），firmly（副詞）

　♪　a firm Buddhist
　　　虔誠的佛教徒

　♪　a soft, medium firm, or firm mattress
　　　一塊軟的、中等硬度或硬的床墊

　♪　All the windows were firmly closed when the typhoon swept across Taiwan.
　　　颱風橫掃台灣時，所有的窗戶都緊緊地關著。

　♪　His request was firmly rejected.
　　　他的請求遭到堅定地拒絕。

7.　be jam-packed with 被……擠得滿滿的

　♪　The balcony was jam-packed with plants.
　　　陽台上滿是盆栽。

8.　middle age 中年（大約是40歲到60歲）

　♪　People tend to put on weight in middle age.
　　　人到中年比較容易發胖。

形容詞 middle-aged 中年的

☞ <u>Middle-aged</u> women tend to put on weight.
　中年婦人很容易發福。

9. 「none of + 複數名詞」為表否定的用法,中文常解釋為「(都)沒有,(都)不是」,後面可接單數動詞(美式英文居多)或複數動詞(英式英文居多),如文中的...none of them <u>were</u> my friends. 在英式英文中則常寫作...none of them <u>was</u> my friends.

10. shall 常在英式英文中出現,美式英文則常用 should 或 will 取代 shall。這句用 should或shall都可以,但shall 通常只與 I 或 we 相連,如:

☞ I shall know more next week.
　下星期我會知道得更多。

☞ We shall go right now.
　我們現在就走。

11. gym 健身房或體育館

☞ I often work out in the school <u>gym</u>.
　我常在學校體育館運動健身。

☞ This private <u>gym</u> has a steam room and a sauna.
　這家私人健身房有蒸氣室和烤箱。

12. take off 是「脫掉(衣物等)」,其反義片語為 put on「穿上或戴上(衣物等)」。

8-5-1 選選看哪一個答案最適合：

1. He _____ be the one who stole the money.

    (a) has better　(b) have to　(c) could

2. She _____ get upset if you don't tell her the truth.

    (a) may　(b) had better　(c) have to

3. I _____ speak Mandarin when I was a kid.

    (a) can　(b) could　(c) have to

4. Mary _____ be in Taipei by now.

    (a) would have　(b) should　(c) had to

5. John _____ be upset if you don't answer his e-mail.

    (a) must to　(b) had better　(c) will

6. _____ I have something to drink?

    (a) Had　(b) Am　(c) Could

7. I have some free time. I _____ help him right now.

    (a) can　(b) has to　(c) had to

8. I _____ drive her car when she is out of town.

    (a) would　(b) can　(c) could

9. _____ you give me a ride to school(載我去學校)?

    (a) May　(b) Shall　(c) Can

10. You _____ look good for your interview if you want to get that job.

    (a) may　(b) shall　(c) had better

11. I am not sure where she is. She _____ be playing computer games in her room.

    (a) had better　(b) migh　t(c) would

12. Mom _____ have returned the book I borrowed from the library. I couldn't find it.

    (a) shall　(b) will　(c) must

13. You _____ be rich to be a success.（成功不見得要有錢。）

    (a) can't　(b) shouldn't　(c) don't have to

14. You _____ get the job if you don't speak English fluently.

    (a) must　(b) had better　(c) can't

15. You had better bring some cash（現鈔）. The restaurant _____ not accept the credit card.

    (a) should　(b) must　(c) may

16. I _____ take care of everything for you.

    (a) will　(b) has to　(c) would

17. Sometimes I am not as confident as I _____ be.

    (a) would　(b) should　(c) has to

18. You _____ allow your child to swim alone in the pool. It's dangerous.

    (a) should　(b) might not　(c) must not

19. This test _____ be a little bit too difficult for me. May I try another one?

    (a) could　(b) must not　(c) has to

20. Next time I _____ try your steamed fish.

    (a) may be　(b) may　(c) must to

8-5-2 請選出最適當的助動詞填入空格中，有的空格甚至可以填三到四個答案，注意，有些字的第一個字母要改為大寫：

can't,　might as well,　could,　must be,　have to,　must,　might,　should,　may,　will

1. ＿＿＿＿＿＿ I ask how old you are?

2. I ＿＿＿＿＿＿ be 55 at the end of this year.

3. You ＿＿＿＿＿＿ be 55. You look like someone in her 30s.

4. I ＿＿＿＿＿＿ tell you the truth. 55 is not my correct age.

5. Now you ＿＿＿＿＿ tell me exactly how old you are. I have to write it down.

6. I ＿＿＿＿＿＿ be wrong, but I remember my mom told me I was born in 1962.

7. Let me see, if I counted correctly you ＿＿＿＿＿＿ be 45 this year.

8. You ＿＿＿＿＿＿ have thought I was younger if I hadn't told you.

9. Since you have to wait, you ＿＿＿＿＿＿ sit down and relax.

10. You ＿＿＿＿＿＿ Kevin's brother. You have the same eyes.

8-5-3 問答

1. Why did his mom call him from behind?

   She called him because ＿＿＿＿＿＿＿＿＿＿＿＿＿＿＿＿＿＿＿＿＿

2. Where could he buy the milk?

   He ＿＿＿＿＿＿＿＿＿＿＿＿＿＿＿＿＿＿＿＿＿＿＿＿＿＿＿＿＿＿

3. How did he get to the school basketball courts?

   He got there ＿＿＿＿＿＿＿＿＿＿＿＿＿＿＿＿＿＿＿＿＿＿＿＿

4. Was he willing to help his mom?

   ＿＿＿＿＿＿＿＿＿＿＿＿＿＿＿＿＿＿＿＿＿＿＿＿＿＿＿＿＿＿

5.   Were there many people at the school basketball courts?

_____

6.   Could he find his friends among many basketball players?

_____

7.   Who waved to him while he was looking for his friends?

_____

8.   Where were his friends?

They _____

9.   What did he see inside the gym?

He _____

10. What did he do before joining the game?

He _____

8-5-4 改錯

1.   He may be choose this book to read.

2.   She has better send an e-mail to her boss right now.

3.   He must to finish his homework by 9:00.

4.   This can be your pen. It has my name on it.

5.   It's too late. You had better not to go tonight.

6.   I would go to the convenience store tomorrow.

7.   He had to tidies up his room before he leaves.

8.   You must to be tired after standing for so long.

9.   If I visit Nantou, I would buy some tea.

10. You had to pay me right now, or I will charge you more.

11. We are reluctantly to join the game.

12. Many middle-age men don't care about their health.

8-5-5 英文該怎麼寫？

1. 她看起來很像你，所以她一定是你的姊妹。

   _____

2. 你明天可不可以在體育館後面等我？

   _____

3. 你最好明天發個簡訊給他。

   _____

4. 他剛穿上了夾克，又很快脫掉了。

   _____

5. 她的臥房裡堆滿了瓶子。

   _____

6. 他心不甘情不願地去便利商店買牛奶。

   _____

7. 回家的路上，我遇到一位籃球員。

   _____

8. 那位中年女性一定是你的英文老師。

   _____

9. 飯前你最好洗手，否則可能會生病。(Before meals, ...)

   _____

10. 所有熟面孔中間，我找不到任何一個我的同班同學。(Among all the...)

   _____

答案請見 pp. 168-170

 朗讀 CD 第 25 軌

 互動光碟

附錄

不規則動詞三態變化表

I. 三態同形（動詞原形、過去式、過去分詞完全相同）

動詞原形	過去式	過去分詞	現在分詞
burst 爆裂、突然……	burst	burst	bursting
cost 值、花(多少錢)	cost	cost	costing
cut 切、剪、割	cut	cut	cutting
hit 打擊、到達	hit	hit	hitting
hurt 受傷	hurt	hurt	hurting
let 讓	let	let	letting
put 放	put	put	putting
quit 停止	quit	quit	quitting
read 讀	read	read	reading
set 安置	set	set	setting
shut 關	shut	shut	shutting
spread 展開	spread	spread	spreading

*注意：read的過去式和過去分詞拼法與動詞原形一樣，但發音不同。

II. 一、三態相同（動詞原形、過去分詞相同）

動詞原形	過去式	過去分詞	現在分詞
become 成為	became	become	becoming
come 來	came	come	coming
overcome 克服	overcame	overcome	overcoming
run 跑	ran	run	running

III. 二、三態相同（過去式、過去分詞相同）

動詞原形	過去式	過去分詞	現在分詞
bring 帶來	brought	brought	bringing
build 建造	built	built	building
buy 買	bought	bought	buying
catch 接住、捉到	caught	caught	catching
deal 處理	dealt	dealt	dealing
dig 挖	dug	dug	digging
feed 餵	fed	fed	feeding
feel 覺得	felt	felt	feeling
fight 爭吵	fought	fought	fighting
find 找到	found	found	finding
hang 掛	hung	hung	hanging
have(has) 有	had	had	having
hear 聽	heard	heard	hearing
hold 握住	held	held	holding
keep 保持	kept	kept	keeping
lay 置放	laid	laid	laying
lead 引導、領導	led	led	leading
leave 離開	left	left	leaving

lose 遺失	lost	lost	losing
make 使、做	made	made	making
mean 意指	meant	meant	meaning
meet 遇到	met	met	meeting
pay 付錢	paid	paid	paying
say 說	said	said	saying
seek 尋找	sought	sought	seeking
sell 賣	sold	sold	selling
send 寄、送	sent	sent	sending
shine 發光	shone	shone	shining
sit 坐	sat	sat	sitting
sleep 睡	slept	slept	sleeping
spend 花(時間、金錢)	spent	spent	spending
stand 站	stood	stood	standing
teach 教	taught	taught	teaching
tell 告訴	told	told	telling
think 想	thought	thought	thinking
understand 了解	understood	understood	understanding
win 贏	won	won	winning

IV. 一、二、三態各不相同（動詞原形、過去式、過去分詞各不相同）

動詞原形	過去式	過去分詞	現在分詞
be 是	was/were	been	being
begin 開始	began	begun	beginning
blow 吹	blew	blown	blowing

break 打破	broke	broken	breaking
choose 選擇	chose	chosen	choosing
do（does）做	did	done	doing
drink 喝	drank	drunk	drinking
drive 開車	drove	driven	driving
eat 吃	ate	eaten	eating
fall 落下	fell	fallen	falling
fly 飛	flew	flown	flying
forbid 禁止	forbade	forbidden	forbidding
forget 忘記	forgot	forgotten	forgetting
forgive 原諒	forgave	forgiven	forgiving
freeze 結冰、使凍住	froze	frozen	freezing
get 拿	got	gotten	getting
give 給與	gave	given	giving
go 走	went	gone	going
grow 生長	grew	grown	growing
hide 藏	hid	hidden	hiding
know 知道	knew	known	knowing
lie 躺	lay	lain	lying
mistake 弄錯、誤解、 把……誤認為	mistook	mistaken	mistaking
ride 騎	rode	ridden	riding
ring 響	rang	rung	ringing
rise 升起、起床	rose	risen	rising
see 看	saw	seen	seeing

shake 搖動	shook	shaken	shaking
sing 唱	sang	sung	singing
speak 說	spoke	spoken	speaking
steal 偷	stole	stolen	stealing
swim 游泳	swam	swum	swimming
take 拿去	took	taken	taking
tear 撕開、撕裂	tore	torn	tearing
throw 丟、擲	threw	thrown	throwing
wake 醒來	woke	waken	waking
wear 穿	wore	worn	wearing
write 寫	wrote	written	writing

總複習

I. 選擇題

1. He finally finished _____ his paper.

    (a)writing　(b)write　(c)to write

2. I spent an hour _____ for driving lessons.

    (a)to sign up　(b)sign up　(c)signing up

3. Dad's words didn't discourage Mom. Instead, they _____ her will to continue learning.

    (a)strength　(b)strengthening　(c)strengthened

4. My dad is used to _____ flip-flops at home.

    (a)wear　(b)wearing　(c)wears

5. Her life is far different from her _____ husband's.

    (a)retire　(b)retired　(c)retiring

6. His endless _____ is driving me crazy.

    (a)nag　(b)nagging　(c)nagged

7. Today I _____ my teacher in the park.

    (a)showed up　(b)put on　(c)ran into

8. After hanging _____ the phone, Mom asked me to make my bed.

    (a)on　(b)up　(c)for

9. As I was about to dig in, Mom _____ me to wait.

    (a)registered　(b)retreated　(c)reminded

10. There is a great exhibition(展覽)at the art museum. Let's go and check it
    _____.
    (a)out (b)in (c)up

11. He often _____ down and falls asleep right away.
    (a)lays (b)lies (c)lying

12. I _____ uncomfortable sitting on this old couch.
    (a)fell (b)feeling (c)felt

13. He _____ deeply and evenly when he sleeps.
    (a)breath (b)brcathing (c)breathes

14. I _____ history as my major.
    (a)choice (b)chose (c)choosing

15. They suggested I _____ abroad (留學)after graduating from college.
    (a)study (b)studied (c)studying

16. He found lots of information _____ the Internet.
    (a)on (b)in (c)at

17. To my _____, no one showed up.
    (a)disappoint (b)disappointing (c)disappointment

18. The place under the dining table has become _____ spot in the house.
    (a)dirty (b)dirtier (c)the dirtiest

19. To my surprise, something _____ happened.
    (a)terribly (b)terrible (c)usually

20. This short story is _____ than that one.
    (a)bad (b)interesting (c)worse

21. You have to study _____, or you will fail the test.
    (a)hardly (b)hard (c)more hardly

22.   He did it _____ this time.

(a)careful   (b)more careful   (c)more carefully

23.   I _____ called Mom to come and take a look at Dad and Inky.

(a)secret   (b)secretly   (c)secretive

24.   Because of the cat, they won't get _____ for a while.

(a)boring   (b)bore   (c)bored.

25.   She can run as _____ as her brother.

(a)fast   (b)faster   (c)fastest

26.   He started to drive _____ after getting a ticket.

(a)more slow   (b)more slowly   (c)slower

27.   He _____ send a text message to you.

(a)maybe   (b)may   (c)must be

28.   They _____ be here before we start dinner.

(a)have better   (b)would   (c)had better

29.   I can't find my friends. I _____ sit here and wait.

(a)must to   (b)maybe   (c)may as well

30.   I _____ like to have a cup of black tea.

(a)would   (b)will   (c)must

II. 填充題

1.   My mom _____ (teach)kids for almost 25 years.

2.   She is planning her _____ (retire)step by step.

3.   She visited the community college and _____ (sign up)for a few classes.

4.   _____ (除了)science fiction, she likes all kinds of novels.

5.   When I'm not studying, I have _____ (a little/a few一些)free time to hang out with friends.

6. She avoids _____ (go) out late at night.

7. I had trouble _____ (find) my way back home.

8. _____ (watch) talk shows on TV is her favorite pastime.

9. He often _____ (trick) people, which upsets them.

10. She _____ (write) 10 novels since she _____ (write) her first one at 15 years of age. Now she _____ (write) her 11th one.

11. She _____ (take) her stuffed animal to school yesterday.

12. I _____ (feel) there was something wrong with my stomach (胃) the day before yesterday.

13. The poster _____ (be hung) on the wall for 3 years.

14. His stubbornness (頑固) _____ (lead) to his divorce.

15. Last night I _____ (hear) him play the violin.

16. You go first. I will catch up _____ you later.

17. When my grandma came to visit us, we picked her _____ at the bus station.

18. Chicken soup is a home _____ for colds (感冒).

19. When I called out, Dad _____ (rise) from the bed.

20. The Lins have _____ (raise) three kittens.

21. I spent _____ time than you finishing this project. (= I didn't spend as much time as you.)

22. He is more considerate than I _____.

23. They have more confidence than we _____.

24. Dad and the cat are running _____ (happy) around the living room.

25. He sang _____ (surprise) well this time.

26. I _____ (desperate) need your help.

27. Instead of standing here waiting for them, I _____ as well go join the game. （與其站著乾等，不如加入比賽。）

28. She _____ play at least three instruments.

29. "I will try to be home before dinner starts." I said _____ (reluctant).

30. You must _____ your shoes before entering a Japanese house.

III. 改錯（有些句子有兩個錯誤）

1. The show maybe end at the end of August. I had better check it out now.

2. You must to buy a bottle of soymilk now, or we won't have anything to drink for breakfast.

3. She showed reluctant to lend him the money.

4. That was the work he finished the most careful.

5. Mom was really surprising when she saw the text message.

6. The corner of the kitchen has become dirtiest spot in our house.

7. Dad has lied on the couch the whole morning.

8. If you don't brush your teeth right after each meal, you will have bad breathe.

9. He gave me some advises, but none of them was useful.

10. Play online games have affected his studies.

11. Let me take look the photos you took in Seoul（首爾）.

12. To my surprise, his mom likes to listen hip hop music.

13. She is the delight person that I have ever met.

14. I am used to eat my own packed lunch（自帶便當）instead of have a bite to eat at a roadside stand.

15. The more he trying to discouraging me, the more I want to do it.（他愈試圖阻止我，我就愈想做。）

16. Collect stuffed animals are my hobby.

17. We had great fun to stay in my uncle's house.

18. Except the guitar, she can play many other instruments.

19. What is your car registrate number?

20. If you try a little more times, you will pass the exam.

IV. 翻譯

1. 我現在大四，明年將畢業 (graduate)。

   _____

2. 除了駕駛課，我什麼課都沒報名 (sign up for)。

   _____

3. 他昨天穿了一件背心、短褲和夾腳脫鞋。

   _____

4. 她的生活跟她退休丈夫的不同。

   _____

5. 他以前是(used to)公務員，但現在退休了。

   _____

6. 他花大部分時間待在家裡。

   _____

7. 看綜藝節目(variety shows)是他最喜歡的消遣。

   _____

8. 他正坐在舒服的沙發(couch)上讀雜誌(magazine)。

   _____

9. 抽菸在我家不被允許 (be not allowed)。（我家不准抽菸）

   _____

10. 沒有媽媽唸他，他可以整天躺在床上。（Without...）

_____

11. 掛上電話以後，他命令我們整理我們的房間。（After...）

_____

12. 蒸餃（steamed dumplings）是最好吃（delicious）的食物。

_____

13. 大人們正在交換家傳祕方。（The adults...）

_____

14. 媽媽幫我移除掉（get rid of）電腦遊戲程式。

_____

15. 我們的親戚在我家住了一晚。

_____

16. 媽媽一眼就愛上了那隻流浪貓。

_____

17. 爸爸搭建（set up）了一間專用廁所給小貓咪。

_____

18. 我不情願地退到（retreat）我的臥房去。

_____

19. 顯然地，他已經發了短訊給你。

_____

20. 他是個退了休的中年男人。

_____

答案請見 pp. 171-173

習題解答

第一課　詞類變化──名詞

1-5-1 選選看

1. b　2. c　3. c　4. a　5. b
6. c　7. a　8. a　9. c　10. b
11. c　12. a　13. c　14. b　15. a

1-5-2 填填看

1. little
2. a few
3. little
4. few
5. a little
6. a few
7. little
8. a few
9. a few
10. little
11. a little
12. a little
13. little
14. a little
15. a few

1-5-3 問答

1. Yes, she is.
2. No, she won't.
3. No, she isn't.
4. She has been teaching for 25 years.
5. They're elementary school students.
6. She's planning her retirement .
7. She visited the community college near their home.
8. She registered right away.
9. She signed up for driving lessons.
10. She wanted to get a driver's license.
11. He laughed because she doesn't have any sense of direction.
12. His mom said, "Wait and see", then turned her back to his dad and walked away.

1-5-4 英文該怎麼寫？

1. I learn English step by step.
2. My parents are retired.（My parents have retired.）

3. I take courses every summer at the community college.

4. After he retired, he taught math at the community college.

5. Have you taken driving lessons (before)？

6. My cousins are all elementary school students.

7. My cousin is in the third grade. (My cousin is a third-grader.)

8. Is there a driving school near your home?

9. Does this letter need to be registered?

10. Did you sign up for the cooking class yesterday?

第二課　詞類變化──動名詞

2-5-1 選選看

1. c　2. a　3. b　4. c　5. c
6. a　7. c　8. c　9. b　10. c
11. c　12. b　13. b　14. b　15. a

2-5-2 填填看

1. Going
2. to swim
3. going
4. writing
5. to forgive
6. reading
7. lending
8. winning
9. telling
10. Selling
11. cooking
12. to drive
13. to sleep
14. sleeping
15. going

2-5-3 問答

1. No, they didn't.
2. Yes, she will.
3. Yes, he is.
4. He has been retired for a year.
5. He was a civil servant.
6. Yes, he is.
7. Usually he gets up at nine o'clock in the morning.
8. If he doesn't make breakfast for himself, he has a bite to eat at a roadside stand.
9. He wears flip-flops.
10. He likes to watch talk shows on TV.
    (He likes watching...)
    (Watching talk shows on TV is his favorite pastime.)

2-5-4 改錯

1. He is tying his shoe laces.

2. She goes <u>swimming</u> almost every day.

3. Their <u>laughing</u> at her upset her.

4. I like <u>to send</u>（I like <u>sending</u>）text messages to my friends.

5. She is not used to <u>going</u> out at night.

6. <u>Playing</u> badminton is her favorite activity.

7. I spent all my energy <u>doing</u> this project.

8. We couldn't help <u>crying</u> when we heard the bad news.

9. We will never let ourselves be <u>discouraged</u>.

10. They tried to <u>strengthen</u> their belief in God.

2-5-5 英文該怎麼寫？

1. The pastime I enjoy most is reading English novels.（My favorite pastime is reading English novels.）

2. My father（Dad）is used to getting up early.

3. Don't discourage me from studying English.

4. I used to teach English in a community college.

5. My interest is different from his.（My interests are different from his.）

6. My sister has been retired for three years.

7. He's having a bite to eat at a roadside stand.

8. She gets up at six o'clock every morning.

9. Collecting comic books is my hobby.

10. He's wearing flip-flops and eating at a roadside stand.

第三課　動詞——三態變化

3-5-1 選選看
1. b　2. c　3. b　4. b　5. a
6. c　7. b　8. b　9. c　10. c
11. a　12. b　13. c　14. a　15. a

3-5-2 填填看
1. smoke, quit
2. seen
3. nagged
4. sat
5. known
6. known
7. smell
8. heard
9. came
10. drunk

11. worked（been working）
12. sat
13. felt
14. fell
15. read

3-5-3 問答

1. He heard his dad come home.
2. He saw his dad holding a cup of soymilk in his hand and carrying the newspaper on his head.
3. He was reading the newspaper.
4. He smelled smoke.
5. He was smoking in the living room.
6. His wife（the writer's mom）has told him many times to quit smoking.
7. Yes, he is.
8. No. he hasn't.
9. The writer's mom nags him.
10. They are going to have a big fight.（They will fight.）

3-5-4 改錯

1. He is always <u>bothering</u> me when I am working on my essays.
2. We <u>must take</u> a trip to Korea together.
3. I <u>have known</u> him since he was a little boy.
4. This book was <u>written</u> by a famous author.
5. She has <u>brought</u> many books home.
6. I heard the baby <u>cry</u> last night.
7. Last night she <u>showed</u> me a beautiful picture.
8. Could you <u>hold</u> this for me for a minute?
9. She often <u>teaches</u> her daughter math.
10. This movie was not <u>chosen</u> by me.

3-5-5 英文該怎麼寫？

1. As I was watching TV, I heard a strange sound.
2. Through the window, I saw a child running.
3. He always sits on that comfortable couch and listens to music.（He always sits on that comfortable couch listening to music.）
4. I smell（I smelled）a strange smell.
5. He bought three bottles of soymilk this morning.

6. I'm not used to smoking（cigarettes）.
7. This couple has been arguing （has argued） for 30 years.
8. Her husband is a stubborn person （man）. （Her husband is stubborn.）
9. When I am working on essays, my sister likes to nag me.
10. I've（already）told them many times to quit fighting.

第四課　動詞──動詞片語

4-5-1 填填看
1. grandmother
2. cousin
3. son-in-law
4. cousin
5. brother-in-law
6. niece
7. uncle
8. cousin
9. parents-in-law（in-laws）
10. sister-in-law
11. granddaughter
12. daughter-in-law
13. nephew
14. cousins
15. uncle
16. mother-in-law
17. niece
18. grandparents
19. cousin
20. grandchildren

4-5-2 選擇適當的詞填入空格中
1. listen to
2. get along
3. home remedy
4. tidy up
5. showed up
6. check out
7. dig in
8. put up with
9. running out of
10. lose weight

4-5-3 問答
1. Mom picked up the phone and answered it.
2. She ordered the writer's dad and the writer to tidy up the house.
3. They would visit them on the weekend.
4. The writer's cousins showed up at the door first.
5. They were carrying bags of food in their hands.

6. His home-made foods are taro cakes and steamed Taiwanese Sticky Rice.
7. His mom reminded him to wait.
8. They checked out his latest computer game.
9. They exchanged home remedies.
10. She told him how to quit smoking.

4-5-4 改錯

1. Her mother looks after her children.
2. I can't put up with her any more.
3. You shouldn't look down on your little sister.
4. I will take care of your dog when you are away.
5. When he ran out of money, he came home.
6. I like this delightful music.
7. He has lost a lot of weight.
8. Every time I say something, she copies me.
9. You must pick her up at 4 o'clock at the High Speed Rail Station.
10. They always exchange the latest news.(They are always exchanging the latest news.)

4-5-5 英文該怎麼寫？

1. Every time she calls, I don't feel like answering.
2. Right after hanging up the phone, he turned on the television to watch a talk show.
3. Mom reminded me to visit my teacher on the weekend.
4. Among the colors red, blue, and white, my favorite is white.
5. My cousin is sitting on the comfortable couch eating taro cake.
6. He has tried all kinds of home remedies to lose weight.
7. I don't know when he will show up.
8. They're discussing the bad effects of watching television on children.
9. My aunts are exchanging home remedies.
10. His mother-in-law ordered him to tidy up (clean) his room.

第五課　動詞——容易混淆的動詞

5-5-1 選選看

1. b　2. c　3. c　4. b　5. a
6. b　7. a　8. c　9. c　10. c
11. b　12. b　13. c　14. a　15. b

5-5-2 填填看

1. advice
2. raised
3. rise
4. advised
5. affect
6. hung
7. effects
8. lay
9. lie
10. hang

5-5-3 問答

1. They stayed for one night.
2. They lay down on the bed and chatted about the fun parts of the visit.
3. He had to finish a report about the good effects of the Internet in the modern world.
4. When he turned on his computer, nothing showed up (appeared/ happened) on the screen.
5. His father did.
6. He got rid of some of the computer game programs.
7. He complained that his son spends too much time playing computer games.
8. He advised him to quit playing.
9. He lied to him about using the computer to do homework.
10. It will affect his life and his studies.

5-5-4 改錯

1. She is <u>lying</u> on the bed reading a novel.
2. I <u>felt</u> that she didn't lie to me.
3. Which book did you <u>choose</u>?
4. He <u>hung</u> his shirt on the balcony a week ago.
5. We have to <u>adapt</u> ourselves to the modern world.
6. Losing weight has had some bad <u>effects</u> on her health.
7. She gave me a lot of good <u>advice</u>.
8. Our boss never listens to our <u>complaints</u>.
9. We visited Hualian and <u>stayed</u> in a cheap hotel for three days.

10. They <u>lent</u> a book to me and asked me to return it in three days.

5-5-5 英文該怎麼寫？

1. They are lying on the bed (in bed) listening to music.
2. I stayed at a (my) friend's house for two nights.
3. He gave me a lot of useful advice.
4. I raised my hand to answer the question.
5. I borrowed NT$ 100 from him.
6. He chose this English novel to read.
7. Playing computer games affects my work.
8. I turned on my computer, but nothing appeared on my screen.
9. Finally, our relatives fell asleep.
10. My aunt advised me to quit playing computer games.

第六課 形容詞

6-5-1 選選看

1. c   2. b   3. c   4. b   5. c
6. a   7. c   8. c   9. a   10. c
11. c   12. a   13. b   14. c   15. c

6-5-2 選出適當的形容詞填入句子中

1. private
2. next door
3. expensive
4. fluffy
5. adorable
6. difficult
7. comfortable
8. messy
9. crowded
10. sticky

6-5-3 問答

1. She is the writer's next door neighbor.
2. She showed them a fluffy black stray cat.
3. She found it in a quiet alley nearby.
4. Its fur is as black as ink.
5. She has three cats.
6. Its name is Inky.
7. They named it Inky because its fur is as dark as Ink.
8. She used boxes and old towels to make a comfortable bed for the cat.
9. The space under the dining table became Inky's messy playground.

10. He was angry because the space under the dining table became the dirtiest spot in the house.

6-5-4 改錯

1. You always <u>mess up</u> the living room after I tidy it up.
2. I tried <u>as hard as I possibly could</u> to learn English.
3. I am not <u>as tall as</u> she is.
4. She is <u>the smartest</u> in our family.
5. Taipei 101 is <u>the highest</u> building in Taiwan.
6. The teacher <u>was dissatisfied with</u> students' performance.
7. My grandma is <u>healthier</u> than before.
8. To open the door without knocking is very <u>impolite</u>.
9. The apartment has become very <u>crowded</u>.
10. This towel is <u>drier</u> than that one.

6-5-5 英文該怎麼寫？

1. I picked up a stray cat in the park.
2. I am fond of that fluffy white dog.
3. He showed me that small and quiet study.
4. My next door neighbor is noisy.
5. This dining table is not as long as that one.
6. This is the most comfortable bed in our store.
7. I spend as much time as him studying English.
8. He can't stand his son's messy room.
9. I can only afford that cheaper computer.
10. Although I fell in love with that stray dog at first sight, I can't keep it.

第七課　副詞

7-5-1 選選看

1. b　　2. c　　3. a　　4. c　　5. c
6. b　　7. c　　8. b　　9. c　　10. a
11. c　12. c　13. a　14. b　15. b

7-5-2 問答

1. Dad played with Inky.
2. He had Inky chase a small rubber ball.
3. Come here, Inky. Catch the ball.
4. Dad's soft side.

5. They retreated to the kitchen.
6. Jie Ming, his junior high school classmate, called him.
7. Jie Ming and a bunch of friends were waiting for him at the school basketball courts.
8. Inky is the common interest of the writer's parents.

7-5-3 改錯

1. Her graduation speech was <u>surprisingly</u> good.
2. Something <u>terrible</u> happened this morning.
3. I <u>hung</u> up the phone and ran over to meet her.
4. We <u>quickly</u> retreated to a safer place.
5. He easily <u>gets</u> <u>bored</u>.
6. I can't help <u>feeling</u> sorry for the poor guy.
7. I felt <u>terribly</u> sorry about the incident.
8. He hid his diary at the <u>secret</u> location.
9. I will meet a bunch of <u>friends</u> to play basketball.
10. If she drives more <u>slowly</u>, I will be able to catch up with her.

7-5-4 英文該怎麼寫？

1. I put on my shorts and sneakers to (go) play basketball.
2. Something terrible happened; I had to leave quickly.
3. He quietly retreated to his bedroom.
4. He drives as slowly as his brother.
5. I secretly hid the stray cat under my desk.
6. Obviously, he doesn't want to hear what you have to say. (Obviously, he didn't want to hear what you said.)
7. I checked the text message. It was from my cousin.
8. Actually, I don't like this latest computer game.
9. He is comfortably sitting on the couch reading a novel.
10. He thoughtfully gave me a cup of soy milk.

第八課 助動詞

8-5-1 選選看哪一個答案最適合

1. c　2. a　3. b　4. b　5. c
6. c　7. a　8. b　9. c　10. c
11. b　12. c　13. c　14. c　15. c
16. a　17. b　18. c　19. a　20. b

8-5-2 請選出最適當的助動詞填入空格中，有的空格甚至可以填三到四個答案，注意，有些字的第一個字母要改為大寫

1. Could, Might, May,

2. will,

3. can't

4. must, should, have to

5. have to, should, must,

6. could, might, may

7. could, have to, must, should,

8. might,

9. might as well, should,

10. must be

8-5-3 問答

1. She called him because she wanted him to buy a bottle of milk (on his way back home).

2. He could buy the milk at a convenience store.

3. He got there by scooter.

4. No, he wasn't. He was reluctant.

5. Yes, the school basketball courts were jam-packed.

6. No, he couldn't.

7. Jie Ming waved to him.

8. They were in the indoor basketball court.

9. He saw many familiar faces.

10. He took off his jacket.

8-5-4 改錯

1. He may choose this book to read.

2. She had better send an e-mail to her boss right now.

3. He must finish his homework by 9:00.

4. This can't be your pen. It has my name on it.

5. It's too late. You had better not go tonight.

6. I will go to the convenience store tomorrow.

7. He has to tidy up his room before he leaves.

8. You must be tired after standing for so long.

9. If I visit Nantou, I will buy some tea.

10. You have to pay me right now, or I will charge you more.

11. We are reluctant to join the game.

12. Many middle-aged men don't care about their health.

8-5-5 英文該怎麼寫？

1. She looks like you very much, so she must be your sister.

2. Can you wait for me behind the gym tomorrow?

3. You had better send him a text message tomorrow.
4. He put on his jacket and took it off right away.
5. Her bedroom is jam-packed with bottles.
6. He reluctantly went to the convenience store to buy milk.
7. On my way home, I ran into (met) a basketball player.
8. That middle-aged woman must be your English teacher.
9. Before meals, you had better wash your hands or you might get sick.
10. Among all the familiar faces, I couldn't find any of my classmates.

總複習解答

I. 選擇題

1.(a)	2.(c)	3.(c)	4.(b)	5.(b)
6.(b)	7.(c)	8.(b)	9.(c)	10.(a)
11.(b)	12.(c)	13.(c)	14.(b)	15.(a)
16.(a)	17.(c)	18.(c)	19.(b)	20.(c)
21.(b)	22.(c)	23.(b)	24.(c)	25.(a)
26.(b)	27.(b)	28.(c)	29.(c)	30.(a)

II. 填充題

1. taught/has taught
2. retirement
3. signed up
4. Except for
5. a little
6. going
7. finding
8. Watching
9. tricks
10. has written, wrote, is writing
11. took
12. felt
13. was hung/has been hung
14. led
15. heard
16. with
17. up
18. remedy
19. rose
20. raised
21. less
22. am
23. do
24. happily
25. surprisingly
26. desperately
27. might/may
28. can
29. reluctantly
30. take off

III. 改錯（有些句子有兩個錯誤）

1. The show <u>may</u> end at the end of August. I had better check it out now.
2. You <u>must buy</u> a bottle of soymilk now, or we won't have anything to drink for breakfast.
3. She showed <u>reluctance</u> to lend him the money.
4. That was the work he finished the most <u>carefully</u>.
5. Mom was really <u>surprised</u> when she saw the text message.
6. The corner of the kitchen has become <u>the</u> dirtiest spot in our house.
7. Dad has <u>lain</u> on the couch the whole morning.
    （Dad <u>lay</u> on the couch the whole morning.）
8. If you don't brush your teeth right after each meal, you will have bad <u>breath</u>.
9. He gave me some <u>advice</u>, but none of it was useful.
10. <u>Playing</u> online games <u>has</u> affected his studies.
11. Let me take a look at the photos you took in Seoul（首爾）.
    （Let me look <u>at</u> the photos you took in Seoul.）
12. To my surprise, his mom likes to listen <u>to</u> hip hop music.
13. She is the <u>most</u> <u>delightful</u> person that I have ever met.
14. I am used to <u>eating</u> my own packed lunch（自帶便當）instead of <u>having</u> a bite to eat at a roadside stand.
15. The more he <u>tries</u> to <u>discourage</u> me, the more I want to do it.
16. <u>Collecting</u> stuffed animals <u>is</u> my hobby.
17. We had great fun <u>staying</u> <u>at</u> my uncle's house.
18. In addition to/Besides the guitar, she can play many other instruments.
19. What is your car <u>registration</u> number?
20. If you try a <u>few</u> more times, you will pass the exam.

IV. 翻譯

1. I am now a senior at university and will graduate next year.
2. Except for driving lessons, I did not sign up for any other classes.

3.　Yesterday he wore a tank top, shorts, and flip-flops.

4.　Her life is different from her retired husband's.

5.　He used to be a civil servant, but now he is retired.

6.　He spends most of his time at home.

7.　Watching variety shows is his favorite pastime.

8.　He is sitting on a comfortable couch reading a magazine.

9.　Smoking is not allowed in my house.

10.　Without mom's nagging, he could lie in bed all day.

11.　After hanging up the phone, he ordered us to tidy up our rooms.

12.　Steamed dumplings are the most delicious food.

13.　The adults are exchanging home remedies.

14.　Mom helped me get rid of my computer game programs.

15.　Our relatives stayed at our house for one night.

16.　Mom fell in love with the stray cat at first sight.

17.　Dad set up a private bathroom for the kitten.

18.　I reluctantly retreated to my bedroom.

19.　Obviously, he（has）sent you a text message.
　　（Obviously, he（has）sent a text message to you.）

20.　He's a retired middle-aged man.

Linking English

專門替中國人寫的英文課本 高級本上冊

2023年7月二版 　　　　　　　　　　　　　　　定價：新臺幣350元

有著作權·翻印必究

Printed in Taiwan.

著　　　者	文　庭　澍
策 劃 審 訂	李　家　同
叢 書 主 編	林　雅　玲
校　　　對	呂　淑　美
	漆　聯　榮
封 面 設 計	蔡　婕　岑

出　版　者	聯經出版事業股份有限公司	副 總 編 輯	陳　逸　華
地　　　址	新北市汐止區大同路一段369號1樓	總 編 輯	涂　豐　恩
叢書主編電話	(02)86925588轉5305	總 經 理	陳　芝　宇
台北聯經書房	台北市新生南路三段94號	社　　長	羅　國　俊
電　　　話	(02)23620308	發 行 人	林　載　爵
郵政劃撥帳戶	第0100559-3號		
郵 撥 電 話	(02)23620308		
印　刷　者	世和印製企業有限公司		
總 經 銷	聯合發行股份有限公司		
發　行　所	新北市新店區寶橋路235巷6弄6號2F		
電　　　話	(02)29178022		

行政院新聞局出版事業登記證局版臺業字第0130號

本書如有缺頁，破損，倒裝請寄回台北聯經書房更換。ISBN　978-957-08-7029-9 (平裝附光碟片)

聯經網址 http://www.linkingbooks.com.tw

電子信箱 e-mail:linking@udngroup.com

國家圖書館出版品預行編目資料

專門替中國人寫的英文課本 高級本上冊/
　文庭澍著．李家同策劃審訂．二版．新北市．聯經．2023.07
　184面．19×26公分．（Linking English）
　ISBN　978-957-08-7029-9（平裝附光碟片）
　[2023年7月二版]

　1. CST：英語　2. CST：讀本

805.18　　　　　　　　　　　　　　　　112011054